A Wild Ride Through the Night

Also by Walter Moers

The 13½ Lives of Captain Bluebear

Walter Moers

A Wild Ride through the Night

suggested by twenty-one illustrations
by Gustave Doré

Translated from the German by
John Brownjohn

Secker & Warburg
LONDON

Published by Secker & Warburg 2003

2 4 6 8 10 9 7 5 3 1

First published in Great Britain in 2003 by
Secker & Warburg
Random House, 20 Vauxhall Bridge Road,
London SW1V 2SA

Random House Australia (Pty) Limited
20 Alfred Street, Milsons Point, Sydney,
New South Wales 2061, Australia

Random House New Zealand Limited
18 Poland Road, Glenfield,
Auckland 10, New Zealand

Random House (Pty) Limited
Endulini, 5A Jubilee Road, Parktown 2193, South Africa

The Random House Group Limited Reg. No. 954009
www.randomhouse.co.uk

A CIP catalogue record for this book
is available from the British Library

ISBN 0436220547

Papers used by Random House are natural,
recyclable products made from wood grown in sustainable forests;
the manufacturing processes conform to the environmental
regulations of the country of origin

Typeset in Bembo 12.5/18pt by SX Composing DTP, Rayleigh, Essex
Printed and bound in Great Britain by
Biddles Ltd, Guildford & Kings Lynn

GUSTAVE DORÉ, French painter and illustrator, b. Strasbourg, 6 Jan. 1832, d. Paris, 23 Jan. 1883, displayed an outstanding talent for drawing as a boy and lithographed sketches for a history of manners in his tenth year. He moved to Paris at the age of thirteen and was employed as a caricaturist by the *Journal pour rire* two years later. In 1854 he published his earliest illustrated work, Rabelais' *Gargantua and Pantagruel*. This was only the first of the numerous series that made him one of the most popular, prolific and successful book illustrators of the mid nineteenth century. His inexhaustibly fertile imagination and exceptional facility led ultimately to the grotesque lack of moderation that marred his last major work, the drawings for Ariosto's *Orlando Furioso*.

It was dark when Gustave put to sea. He preferred to travel by night. In any case, visibility seemed unimportant to someone who had no idea where his voyage would take him. The sky was enshrouded in clouds as black as ink. Now and then a star or the moon's pock-marked face would peep forth, shedding just enough light for him to see the ship's wheel in his hands. Gustave had read somewhere that it was possible to get your bearings at sea by observing the position of the stars. He wanted to master that art some day, but at present he had to rely on his instincts.

'Hard-a-port!' he shouted, and spun the wheel to the left. Was 'port' on the left or the right? Did a ship turn right when you turned the wheel to the left, or was it the other way round? Temporarily brushing these questions aside, Gustave spun the wooden wheel vigorously so as to give his crew an impression of grim determination.

'We'll never outrun it, Cap'n!' Dante, his trusty, one-eyed boatswain, had come up behind him. The experienced seaman's voice was trembling with fear. 'We can't possibly outrun it, can we?'

Although Gustave was only twelve, the crew of the *Aventure* looked up to him as if he were a giant—even though they had to bend down to do so. Kneading his cap in his calloused hands, Dante regarded his young skipper with a look of hope in his lone eye. Gustave turned to face the wind and sniffed it. The air was as warm and moist as it tends to be before a violent storm.

'Outrun it?' he called over his shoulder. 'Outrun what, my faithful Dante?'

'The storm, Cap'n! Or rather, the storms.'

'The storm?' said Gustave. 'What kind of storm do you mean?'

'I mean a *Siamese Twins Tornado*, Cap'n. It's hot on our heels, too!' Dante levelled a trembling forefinger at something beyond the ship's stern, and Gustave followed the direction of his gaze. What he saw there was terrifying indeed: two enormous waterspouts had arisen from the sea. Their whirling shafts towered as high as the dark clouds overhead, sucking the water and all its contents into the sky. Roaring like maddened giants, they sped towards the *Aventure* at a rate of knots.

'Oh, so it's a *Siamese Twins Tornado*,' Gustave said in a deliberately casual tone. 'An unpleasant phenomenon, but absolutely no reason for anyone to lose control of his knee joints.' He cast a reproachful glance at Dante's trembling legs.

'Take in sail!' he ordered briskly. 'Steer three—no, four degrees to starboard!' The boatswain pulled himself together and saluted, shamed by his imperturbable young skipper's death-defying composure. 'Aye-aye, Cap'n!' he cried. He clicked his heels and strode off, stiff-legged.

Gustave's own knees did not start knocking until Dante had stalked off. His hands gripped the ship's wheel tightly. A *Siamese Twins Tornado*, eh? Great! The most dangerous natural phenomenon anyone could encounter anywhere on the seven seas! A pair of tornadoes, two meteorological twins who seemed to communicate by telepathic means and hunted ships as a team. If one failed to sink you, the other finished the job.

Gustave looked back at the roaring waterspouts. They seemed to have doubled in size in no time. He could see huge octopuses, whales and sharks being plucked from the sea and hurled through the air. Shafts of lightning darted back and forth between the

gigantic, whirling tornadoes, creating a dazzling white network that lit up the *Aventure* like a ghost ship.

'Ah, so *that's* how they communicate!' Gustave told himself. 'By electricity! I must convey this information to the International Tornado Research Centre without delay—if I survive.'

He looked straight ahead again. 'It doesn't matter a row of beans which way I steer,' he reflected. 'If we go left, the left-hand tornado will get us. If we go right, the right-hand one will.'

This disheartening thought had only just occurred to him when the *Aventure* was borne upwards by a huge wave. For a moment the ship hung almost motionless in the air, poised on its foaming crest. The ocean seemed to pause in its eternal undulations, almost as if it had become the tornadoes' accomplice and were serving up the fleeing ship on a tray of white froth.

'We've come to a standstill,' Gustave thought desperately. 'We're done for!'

At that moment the left-hand tornado seized the *Aventure*, enveloping her in darkness. A fearsome gurgle from the bowels of the ocean drowned every other sound including the sailors' cries of terror. Gustave strapped himself to the ship's wheel with his belt and shut his eyes.

He was prepared to die—prepared to plunge with his ship to the bed of the ocean if the sea-gods so ordained; as her captain, it was his duty to do so. In his mind's eye he could already see his skeleton nibbled clean by fish, still lashed to the wheel of a wreck lying on the seabed with stingrays swimming through its splintered remains.

Then silence fell: not a sound, not a whisper, no motion at all.

Gustave felt as if he were floating, weightless, in space. Only the wheel in his hands reminded him that he had been in the thick of a raging storm just a split second earlier.

'I'm dead,' he thought. 'So that's what it's like: you don't hear a thing any more.' He risked opening his eyes and looked up. Overhead was a kind of enormous funnel, and through it he could see straight into the cosmos, a black disk filled with scintillating stars. Around him was a vortex of sea water, splintered wood and whirling air, all of it being propelled outwards by centrifugal force: Gustave was in the eye of the storm, the zone of absolute stillness in the heart of the tornado.

He watched in horror as the grey tube sucked his men into the sky, but he could only see their gaping mouths and staring eyes, not hear their heart-rending cries.

The *Aventure* was lifted into the air once more. Gustave thought she would soar straight into outer space, but the tornado suddenly detached itself from the surface of the ocean and rose into the air. It released its hold on the ship and whirled skywards, growing thinner and thinner. Closely followed by its twin, it plunged into the dark mass of clouds like an immense serpent composed of sea water, air, sailors, and ship's wreckage. The two storms emitted a last, triumphant bellow from inside the clouds. Then they were gone.

But the *Aventure* herself fell back into the sea. The impact snapped her rigging and made the nails pop out of her planks like bullets. White foam blossomed around her hull as she landed. Timber splintered, sailcloth ripped, anchor chains rattled. Then came silence, absolute silence: the waves had subsided. The ship rocked gently to and fro, sending a few barrels rumbling across the deck, but that was all. The tempest was over as suddenly as it had begun.

Gustave unbuckled himself from the ship's wheel. Still thoroughly bemused, he tottered off on a tour of inspection. The *Aventure* was nothing more than a wreck, her sails in shreds, her hull riddled with holes, her deck bristling with sprung planks like the body of a half-plucked chicken. She was slowly but steadily sinking.

'This is the end,' whispered Gustave.

'Yes . . . "All that comes into being is worthy of perishing,"' replied a voice from the ship's stern. Gustave turned to look. Amid the snapped masts and crazy tangle of rigging he saw a horrific figure perched on the taffrail. It was a skeleton, a man devoid of skin and flesh attired in a voluminous black cloak. His bony hands were holding a casket, his empty eye sockets facing in Gustave's direction.

At his feet knelt a young woman who must once upon a time have been very beautiful. Now, however, her fine features were distorted into a mask of insanity as wild and disordered as her flowing fair hair. She was in the act of rolling two dice across the deck.

'Goethe!' said the skeleton.

'You mean . . . you're Goethe?' Gustave asked, puzzled.

'No, the quotation was from Goethe. I'm Death, and this is Dementia, my poor, mad sister. Say hello, Dementia!'

'I'm not mad!' the young woman retorted in an unpleasantly harsh and strident voice, without interrupting her game of dice.

'And what is your name?' asked Death.

'Gustave,' the boy replied stoutly. 'Gustave Doré.'

'Good,' said Death. 'I'm in the right place, then. I've come to fetch your soul.' He indicated the casket in his hand, which, Gustave now saw, was shaped like a miniature coffin. 'Do you know what this is?'

Gustave shook his head.

'It's a soul-coffin,' Death announced with a touch of pride in his sinister voice. 'Yes indeed! My own invention. I'm not interested in your body. That will either feed the sharks or be dispersed in the ocean by a process of decay as natural as anything ever is on this pitiless planet of ours. I want your soul, just your soul, so that I can burn it.'

'No, he belongs to me!' screeched Dementia, pointing to the dice. Having just thrown a double six for the second time, she scooped them up and threw them again.

'Hm,' Death said sullenly, 'we'll have to see about that.' The dice came to a standstill: a five and a six.

'Five sixes and one five,' sighed Death. 'That's hard to beat.'

'He's mine!' Dementia exclaimed in triumph, and uttered a hysterical laugh. Her glowing eyes flickered nervously as she gazed at Gustave.

'It's like this,' Death explained. 'I'll get you anyway, sooner or later, but if you're *really* unlucky, my esteemed sister will also get a slice of the cake. That means you'll go mad before you die. In your case the process will probably take the following form: you'll spend a few weeks drifting around on a raft until the merciless sun dehydrates your brain and you start seeing water sprites, or maybe your dead grandmother, who'll address you in the voice of your

violin teacher—or something of the kind. And then you'll start to eat yourself alive.'

Death shrugged his shoulders and threw the dice. 'I'm sorry, those ideas aren't mine. That's simply how it is with, er . . . insanity.'

He tapped his skull meaningfully with a bony forefinger, but not before making sure that Dementia was concentrating on the dice as they rolled across the deck. A double six.

'You see?' said Death, 'I'm doing my best for you.' He threw again. Another double six.

'You mean you're playing for *me*?' Gustave ventured at last.

'What else? You don't imagine we'd board a sinking hulk during a *Siamese Twins Tornado* just for a game of dice, do you? It's all or nothing now, my boy.' Death threw the dice for the third time. Another double six came up. He clapped his bony hands with a sound like a bunch of pencils rattling on the lid of a coffin. Dementia uttered a screech that made the hairs on Gustave's neck stand on end.

'I was in luck!' said the skeleton. 'And now, my boy, would you kindly surrender your soul?'

Gustave shuddered. 'Surrender my soul? What do you mean? How am I supposed to do that?'

'*How* you do it is all the same to me.' Death made a dismissive gesture. 'You could jump overboard and drown. You could take one of those ropes and hang yourself. Alternatively, there's a nice, sharp cutlass over there. Ever heard of an admirable Japanese custom known as *seppuku*?'

'You want me to kill myself?'

'But of course, what else? You expect *me* to do it? I'm Death, I'm not a killer.' Dementia greeted her brother's little joke with an exaggeratedly strident laugh.

'What do you plan to do with my soul?' asked Gustave. He wasn't really interested in knowing; he simply wanted to gain a little time.

'Oh, fly into outer space with it and throw it into the sun, the way I do with every other soul,' Death said casually. His supercilious tone became tinged with a trace of compassion. 'Why do you think that thing up there burns so brightly, you silly boy? No sun, no life; no life, no souls; no souls, no sun—that's the everlasting cycle of the univ—ouch!' He looked as indignant as an eyeless skeleton could: Dementia had kicked him hard on the shin.

He clapped a bony hand over his bared teeth. 'Oh, my goodness, now I've given away one of the great mysteries of the universe! Well, never mind, you won't be writing a book about it, will you?'

The sinister siblings laughed mechanically, as if this were one of their stock jokes.

'You mean I can't lodge an appeal or anything?' All the resolution had left Gustave's voice. His question was merely another attempt to delay matters. What was he to do? Jump overboard? That would be tantamount to putting an end to himself, which was just what Death wanted.

Death shook his head, and his cervical vertebrae grated against each other with a sound like grinding gears. 'No, I'm sorry, there's nothing to be done,' he said regretfully.

'Yes!' screeched Dementia. 'Yes, there is!'

'Shut up!' Death hissed at his sister.

'If you spoil things for me,' Dementia snarled back at him, 'I'll tell him!'

'Lunatic!'

'Bag of bones!'

Death turned away and glared sullenly at the sea.

Dementia directed her fiery gaze at Gustave. It seemed to him that her eyes were forever changing shape and colour, like two slowly but steadily revolving kaleidoscopes.

'Of course you can do something, boy. Ask my brother about the *Tasks*!' She laughed with a sound like splintering glass.

'Dementia!' Death cut in. Furiously, he pulled his cloak more tightly around him. Then his shoulders sagged and he bowed his bony skull in resignation.

'Very well,' he sighed. 'There *is* a way, but no one has ever tried it. That's because no one has ever asked me about it. Until *now*, that is.' His voice started to shake with suppressed fury. 'Until my enchanting but sadly rather dim-witted sister took it into her head to—'

'Be careful what you say!' Dementia snarled, pointing her fore-finger at him. Her other hand held the dice in an iron grip, ready to hurl them at her brother's head. Death ground his teeth horribly.

'There are five tasks,' he blurted out.

'Five tasks?' Gustave repeated timidly.

'Now there are *six*!'

Gustave preserved a cowed silence.

'**Task Number One**: You rescue a beautiful damsel from the clutches of a dragon.'

Gustave nodded as if he had been expecting something of the kind.

'**Task Number Two**: You traverse a forest swarming with evil spirits.'

'A forest swarming with evil spirits,' muttered Gustave, trying to memorise every detail.

'Yes,' Death added, 'drawing as much attention to yourself as possible.'

Gustave groaned.

'The third task . . . ' Death thought hard. 'The, er, third task . . . ' he muttered to himself, tapping his skull with his forefinger. Gustave waited on tenterhooks.

The skeletal figure straightened up with a jerk, smitten by a flash of inspiration. '**Task Number Three**: You have to guess the names of three giants.'

'*Three* giants?' Gustave protested. 'Isn't that asking a bit—'

'All right, *five* giants!' snarled the skeleton.

'But I—'

'*Six* giants!' Death brought his fist crashing down on the ship's rail.

Gustave bit his lip and resolved to keep mum in future.

'Task Number Four . . . Number Four . . . er . . . ' Death seemed to be finding it harder and harder to think up new tasks.

'Imagination never was his strong point!' sneered Dementia. 'He can burn souls all right, but as for having a single original thought—'

'**Task Number Four!**' Death interrupted her in a thunderous voice. 'You must bring me a tooth belonging to the Most Monstrous of All Monsters!'

'Consider it done,' said Gustave, bowing his head. 'Anything else you'd like?' he thought defiantly.

'Indeed there is!' Death snapped, so sharply that Gustave gave a jump. Was the Grim Reaper a mind-reader as well?

'The fifth task . . . '

'Monsters, dragons, giants, evil spirits . . . ' thought Gustave. 'There can't be anything harder.'

Death lowered his awesomely deep voice still further. 'Now

listen carefully, my boy, because this is the hardest task of all. **Task Number Five**: You must meet yourself!'

'That's not only hard, it's plain impossible!' thought Gustave, but he didn't dare protest.

Death stood up and gathered the folds of his cloak together.

'After that,' he commanded, clearly relieved to have thought up so many ingenious tasks, 'you'll take yourself off to my house on the moon. I shall be waiting there with my, er, enchanting sister to set you your **sixth and final task**—provided you manage to get there, of course.'

'The moon?' said Gustave, impressed. 'Is that where you live?'

'Yes,' sighed Death. 'It's the only place left where you can get away from people. I used to live in an ice castle at the North Pole, but not even *that's* off the beaten track these days, what with all the visitors—polar research scientists, explorers, ornithologists, meteorologists, and so on. I now live on the shores of the Sea of Tranquillity. Mine is the only house there—the only house anywhere on the moon, to be precise. You can't miss it.'

Dementia sighed too, clearly depressed by the thought of her desolate place of residence. 'Personally,' she confided to Gustave in a whisper, 'I'd sooner have a few people around. Those polar explorers were quite good company, but Old Misery-Guts here . . . '

Death silenced her with an imperious gesture.

'See you on the moon, then,' he commanded. '*Before the night's out!*' he added.

'But they're very difficult tasks,' Gustave said plaintively, scratching his head.

Death nodded. 'That's life for you: completely pointless,' he said in a noticeably milder tone. 'It wears you down by degrees—grinds you to dust like pumice stone. For my own part, and at the risk of seeming self-interested, I'd prefer a nice, quick suicide.'

'What do *you* know of life?' Dementia hissed venomously. Death ignored her gibe and went on, 'Well, Gustave, do you accept my challenge, or would you sooner hang yourself from the yardarm? That would be a convenient and extremely time-saving alternative from every point of view.'

He held out a length of rope and tried—insofar as he could do so without any facial muscles—to give Gustave an encouraging smile.

'No, thanks!' Gustave fended off the rope with both hands. 'I'd rather try the tasks.'

'Very well,' Death said with a sigh. 'You've chosen the hardest, longest and most hopeless course of action.' He tossed the rope over the rail. 'Have it your own way. In that case, you must now go at once to the Island of Damsels in Distress. These days, it's the only place where you'll find beautiful girls in the clutches of fire-breathing dragons.'

Gustave couldn't remember any mention of *fire-breathing* dragons. 'The Island of Damsels in Distress—fine, but my ship's sinking and I don't even know where the island is. How am I supposed to get there?' he asked feebly.

'Why,' said Death, casually clicking his fingers, 'like this!'

Gustave's initial impression was that three far-reaching changes had occurred. In the first place, he was no longer in the company of a skeleton and a lunatic on a sinking ship, but soaring through the air. Secondly, he was wearing a helmet and a suit of silver armour and carrying a lance. And, thirdly, he was riding a creature that seemed to be part lion, part horse, and part eagle.

'Before you ask,' said the creature, 'I'm a gryphon. My job is to take you to the Island of Damsels in Distress. In point of fact, we're already there.'

Below them lay an expanse of delightful, summery countryside. Gustave could make out lush meadows filled with wild flowers, clumps of shady trees, and a crystal-clear stream. Young magpies and other small birds were excitedly snapping at airborne insects as they circled above its banks.

'Are you a servant of Death?' asked Gustave.

'Aren't we all?' was the gryphon's mournful rejoinder.

They flew on in silence for a while.

'So where are the damsels?' Gustave asked at length.

'Don't worry,' the gryphon sighed, 'you'll get to see them soon enough. First, though, I thought you might appreciate a little joyride over the damsel-free part of the island—to recuperate, so to speak. After all, you've only just escaped from a Siamese Twins Tornado, a sinking ship, a bout of insanity, and death by hanging.'

'Many thanks,' said Gustave. 'Very considerate of you.'

'Don't mention it,' said the gryphon. 'Mind you, I must confess I was thinking of myself as well. It's part of my job to help you rescue a damsel from the clutches of a dragon.'

'Glad to hear it. The thing is, I've never rescued a damsel from the clutches of a—'

'Neither have I!' the gryphon broke in, sounding worried. 'Neither have I!'

At that, it flapped its wings so violently that the air went whistling past Gustave's ears. The incongruous pair soared high into the sky.

'Let's go! The sooner we get it over, the better.' The gryphon suddenly banked, heeling over at such an extreme angle that Gustave had to cling to its plumage with all his might to prevent the weight of his armour from pitching him off into space.

'We must make for the coast. That's where most of the damsels hang out. They go there because it's where most of the dragons hang out.'

'But . . . In that case, wouldn't it be wiser of them to keep to the interior of the island?'

'Women are an eternal mystery,' the gryphon retorted.

Gustave could already make out the sea glittering in the distance. The sun hovered high overhead, the air was clear and balmy.

'How come it's midday, and so warm?' Gustave asked. Just now, on board ship, it had been the middle of the night.

'It's always midday in these parts,' the gryphon explained, 'and always summertime. For the damsels' sake.'

'I don't understand.'

'Well, it's midday and summertime so the weather's always nice and warm. The damsels like to go around naked, you see.'

'With nothing on, you mean?' gasped Gustave.

The gryphon turned its head and gave him a conspiratorial wink.

'More or less,' it said. 'Because it's so hot.'

On reaching the coast, the gryphon banked gently to the right, spread its wings to their fullest extent, and allowed the light sea breeze to carry them along the rocky shore. All that Gustave could see below him were precipitous cliffs with green waves exploding into foam as they broke against them, a few small bays, some narrow sandy beaches, and rocks, rocks, and more rocks.

'So where are the damsels?' he asked impatiently.

'*There* are your damsels,' sighed the gryphon. 'Up ahead on the right—and don't fall out of the saddle!'

Gustave could detect nothing among the rocks but some pale dots—nesting seagulls, or so he thought at first, but the nearer they drew the more clearly he discerned that they were a whole bevy of young girls.

And, sure enough, they were all very scantily attired and had beautiful figures. Some wore sarongs or headdresses, but many were completely naked. Gustave gasped.

'Keep holding on tight,' the gryphon called. 'Don't lose your nerve.'

'Help!' cried the girls. 'Please help us, won't you?' And they giggled and tittered and nudged each other in the ribs.

'Don't let them fool you,' the gryphon advised. 'Those are *undragoned* damsels. They're of no interest to us.'

'Really not?' said Gustave. 'Why are they all carrying spears?'

'Because of the dragons, of course. They hunt them.'

'Damsels hunt dragons? I thought it was the other way round.'

'Pah! They hunt them, spear them to death, and then eat them. What's more, they don't let anything go to waste. They skin a dragon, cut the meat into chunks, boil it, and pickle it in brine. Dragon blubber they refine into suntan cream—it's always midday and summertime, remember. They make combs out of the scales and sausages out of the creatures' tongues. They even utilise the eyeballs! Those they boil and—'

'Spare me the details!' Gustave exclaimed. 'But how come this place is called the Island of Damsels in Distress? They don't look very distressed to me.'

'The girls thought up the name themselves, of course. What if they'd called it the Island of Dragon-Devouring Damsels, or the Island of Dragon-Slaying Amazons?' The gryphon emitted a hoarse laugh. 'Then no daring young men would ever come here to rescue them from the dragons' clutches, get it?'

'But you just told me they *hunt* dragons.'

'Yes, but now and then a dragon manages to turn the tables. A girl gets separated from the hunting party, loses her spear or something—and at that very moment the dragon comes along! The stupid creatures make a tremendous song and dance when they manage to capture a girl. They chain her to a rock for days on end, brag about it to their friends, and broadcast the news to all and sundry—whereas, if they were smart, they'd simply gobble her up or convert her into juice, the way she'd have done with them.'

The gryphon sighed. 'And then, right on cue, along comes some snotty-nosed youth in shining armour—sorry, that wasn't a dig at you!—who bumps them off. This place should be called the Island of Dragons in Distress, if you want my opinion. It's even said that dragons are sometimes tamed by damsels for the sake of their milk, which is much in demand as a skin-rejuvenation product.'

'Sounds as if it's no great problem, killing one of these monsters.'

'It isn't. We simply fly there and you have a bit of a go at each other, you and the dragon. It tries to bite your head off, whereupon you run it through the throat with your lance. It's child's play. But that's not the point of your task.'

'Really? So what is?'

'Can't tell you—not allowed to. You'll find that out for yourself soon enough.'

'Yoo-hoo!' called the lovely girls among the rocks. 'Help! Come on, rescue us!' And they giggled and tittered some more, spluttering into their hands with uncontrollable mirth.

Gustave couldn't tear his eyes away from this unusual spectacle. 'What if they really do need help?' he asked.

The gryphon's sole response was to flap its wings vigorously, and the girls were soon no more than a sprinkling of pale dots that might have been mistaken for a colony of seabirds. Gustave almost dislocated his neck, trying to catch a last glimpse of them.

In a kind of daze, he sat astride the huge creature as it flew along the coastline with powerful wing-beats. He had never seen so many naked girls at once. To be more precise, he had never seen even one naked girl before, or not in reality, only in the form of a statue or an oil painting in a museum. And these girls had actually moved!

He was jolted out of his daydreams by the gryphon's voice. 'We're now coming to the island's capital city,' it announced in dramatic tones. 'This is the site of the dragon-processing industry.'

Projecting from the rocky coastline were some slender towers built of dazzling white marble, their outer walls entirely adorned with intricate arabesques, half-reliefs, and tiles bearing geometrical designs. Spacious colonnades traversed deserted halls larger than cathedrals, granite round-towers jutted high into the sky. Dense clouds of white vapour issuing from subterranean shafts made these buildings look as if they were constructed on clouds.

'Is that a fairy palace?' Gustave enquired, awestruck.

'No, it's a dragon-processing plant,' the gryphon replied in a businesslike tone. 'It's where captured dragons are wrung out in dragon-juice presses. The juice is then superheated, sterilised, and canned. Tastes awful, but it's reputed to make you immortal if you drink a glass a day. Sells like hot cakes.'

Gustave had always been fascinated by industrial manufacturing processes. 'Why aren't there any workers to be seen?' he asked.

'Everything's fully automated and technologically state-of-the-art. You're looking at the future, my boy. We're on the threshold of a technological revolution. It won't be long before locomotives are flying us to the moon.'

The moon . . . This reference to the earth's satellite reminded Gustave unpleasantly of his unfinished tasks.

'So when do I find my damsel in distress?'

They were gliding along through a dense cloud of steam. Once out the other side, they found themselves back over open sea.

'It won't be long now,' said the gryphon. 'You see that commotion in the water down there?'

Gustave screwed up his eyes.

'Yes,' he said. 'Shoals? Eddies?'

'No, dragons.'

They flew a little lower—low enough for Gustave to make out

a number of scaly monsters splashing around in the shallows or wriggling across the sun-baked rocks. Creatures of alarming size, they made a powerful, predatory impression and seemed to consist of nothing but muscles, sinews and impenetrable scales. They moved with remarkable speed and grace for their size, both on land and water. Living, invulnerable fighting machines, they were equipped with teeth and claws as big and sharp as sabres. Was he really supposed to fight them with his spindly lance?

'I think . . .' muttered the gryphon, peering at something in the distance, 'I think . . .'

'What?'

'Yes, at last!' the mythical beast cried triumphantly. 'There, dead ahead! A damsel in distress!'

Gustave leant forwards and narrowed his eyes until they were slits. Yes, he could now make out a girl chained to a rock by the ankle.

What was more, wallowing in the foaming waves below her was a dragon at least twenty or thirty feet long, a winged monster with green scales and awe-inspiring claws and teeth.

'Look, the dragon's going to devour her!' Gustave yelled as the creature glided through the waves towards the weeping girl and opened its jaws.

'Nonsense, it's only showing off.'

The gryphon seemed to be right, because the dragon dived just before reaching its prey and wallowed in the waves once more, then raised its hideous head above the water and gave an ear-splitting roar—a display of savagery whose sole purpose was to inspire terror in its captive.

'Still,' said the gryphon, 'we seem to have got here at just the right moment. Let's go. I'd advise you to aim your lance at the beast.'

Gustave lowered his lance and the gryphon went into a nosedive. The dragon, which had scented its attackers long ago, awaited them with fangs bared, snarling and emitting smoke from its gaping jaws.

'You must skewer it before it spits fire!' shouted the gryphon.

Gustave had forgotten all about the dragon's fire-spitting facility. The creature breathed in with a vile, gurgling sound which suggested that it was accumulating vast quantities of viscous saliva.

When they were only a few feet from the dragon's head, the gryphon abruptly used its wings as air brakes and brought them to a sudden halt. Instead of transfixing the dragon's throat, Gustave's lance stopped short of its target by a matter of inches. Quick as lightning, the dragon sank its teeth in the wooden shaft.

The shaft splintered, and Gustave was pitched out of the saddle. He flew through the air, turned several somersaults, and, with a mighty splash, landed on his back in the sea. The air inside his armour kept him afloat for a moment or two, but it soon began to leak out.

The gryphon hovered overhead, flapping its wings with an air of serene indifference.

'Why did you do that?' called Gustave.

'Orders from higher authority,' the mythical beast replied.

'But why don't you come to my rescue?' Gustave gurgled, his mouth already filling with sea water.

'Nothing personal,' the gryphon said apologetically. 'I'm a servant of Death, after all.'

Gustave was sinking. Huge air bubbles exploded round him as the water closed over his head. He sank quickly, but not for very long. Like a silver-plated figurehead, he came to rest on the algae-rich sludge a few feet down. He made no attempt to escape from his perilous predicament. Overcome with leaden fatigue, he felt the sea water gently pressing his eyelids shut.

'I'm tired,' he thought. 'I want to sleep. I've sailed across the sea and been pursued by a Siamese Twins Tornado. I've defied Death and ridden a gryphon. I've seen a great many naked girls and fought a dragon. I've sunk to the bed of the ocean. I want to lie here and sleep.'

The water was warm and made him almost weightless despite the armour that was pinning him down on the seabed. He blinked, about to shut his eyes for ever, when some coloured ribbons floated into his field of vision. He forced his eyelids open with an effort: dancing past his face, as red and luminous as lava, was a jellyfish with hundreds of translucent yellow tentacles.

The creature's movements were so graceful and harmonious, so airy and enchanting, that Gustave felt sure he had never seen anything lovelier. Its transparent body almost imperceptibly pulsated from time to time, and delicate undulations rippled along its glassy tentacles. Forever twisting and turning, rising and falling, cavorting and pirouetting with the utmost grace, it seemed to move in time to voices singing a faint, mournful song in the ocean depths. The sound reminded Gustave of an aeolian harp vibrating in the wind.

'That's not an aeolian harp, that's seahorses neighing.' The jellyfish laughed, and its body shook with gentle convulsions. 'Under water it sounds like music. Nice, don't you think?'

'Who are you?' asked Gustave. In his present situation, a talking jellyfish seemed quite as natural to him as the fact that he was addressing it under water without having to open his mouth.

'I'm *The Last Jellyfish*!' the gelatinous creature replied, describing some calligraphic curlicues with its tentacles.

'You mean you belong to a dying breed of jellyfish?'

'No, I'm merely *the last jellyfish you'll ever see.*' The transparent denizen of the deep gave another laugh. 'You're drowning. *You're* the one who'll soon be extinct.'

'I know. It's this stupid armour.'

'Oh, don't worry,' said the jellyfish, 'dying is quite easy. A door opens and you go inside. It's no big deal.'

'What are you doing here?'

'I told you: I'm The Last Jellyfish. Everyone who's drowning sees me. The sight comes free of charge, like the seahorses' chorus. People who burn to death see butterflies the size of newspapers and hear classical music. Close your eyes.'

Gustave did as he was told. Shutting his eyes, he instantly saw a pair of tall white doors with a bust perched on the lintel above them. The doors slowly opened, and a young woman appeared in the crack between them. Gustave recognised her at once.

It was Dementia, Death's crazy sister, but she didn't look as dishevelled as she had on board the *Aventure*. Her hair was elaborately braided, and her face, no longer convulsed with insanity, wore a thoroughly kind and friendly expression.

'Oh, it's you, Gustave!' she called. 'Do come in.'

'It's always like this when you're drowning,' the jellyfish warbled. 'A touch of mental derangement, a glimpse of the lovely Dementia,

the company of a beautiful jellyfish, and some melodious singing—they make the process of dying less painful, tralala!'

Dementia smiled, and Gustave felt strongly tempted to accept her invitation.

'You shouldn't spurn Death's schizophrenic sister,' purred the jellyfish. 'She can protect you from the worst. Drowning is said to be one of the most unpleasant ways to die.'

But then, floating like a pale moon above and beyond Dementia's braided hair, Gustave caught sight of Death's bony skull. In a flash, all his weariness left him. He opened his eyes wide and shouted, 'No! I'm too young to die! I'm only twelve!' The words, which issued from his helmet in the form of plump air bubbles, went spiralling up to the surface of the sea and burst there unheard.

Gustave's wild struggles churned up the water around him. Once graceful, the jellyfish's movements now looked frantic and awkward. It lurched to and fro, its tentacles became entangled, and its glassy body went all misshapen.

'Blah!' it gurgled indignantly, and, enshrouding itself in a mass of tentacles, it glided off into the dark green depths.

Gustave tried to free himself from his armour. He wrenched at the buckles and leather straps until his breastplate finally came off. He slipped out of his metal greaves, stripped off his brassards, and looked up. The huge dragon was still overhead, forever turning on its own axis like a crocodile tearing at its prey. The long jets of flame it kept emitting made the water seethe. If Gustave emerged from the waves, he could choose between being devoured, ripped to shreds by the creature's claws, burnt to death, or boiled alive. The dragon was thirsting for his blood.

So he resisted the urge to surface at once. Bending down to retrieve his sword, he withdrew it from the scabbard and held it above his head with both hands. Then, bending his knees, he pushed off the seabed with all his might and shot upwards like a swordfish skewering its prey. The blade embedded itself deep in the frenzied dragon's soft underbelly. The huge creature went into even more violent convulsions and let out an ear-splitting roar. The sea around it became tinged with purple liquid.

'Dragon-juice,' thought Gustave as he reached the surface at last. 'Aaah!' he went, greedily sucking in great lungfuls of oxygen. The water, which was still boiling in many places, steamed and gave off hissing bubbles. Gustave paddled around aimlessly, panting hard. The gryphon, flapping its wings at regular intervals, had maintained its position overhead.

'I always hoped things would turn out all right for you,' it called. 'Or does that sound insincere?'

'Too right it does!' Gustave shouted back. 'This was a put-up job. At least get me out of here!'

'I shouldn't really do that,' said the gryphon, 'but I will, all the same.' It swooped down, gripped Gustave by the shoulders, and hauled him out of the water.

'You won't believe me, naturally, but I only wanted to save you from a worse fate. Another few minutes, and you'll wish you were back on the seabed.'

'Don't talk nonsense!' snapped Gustave. 'What do you mean?'

'I already told you: fighting the dragon is the pleasanter part of the task.'

Gustave declined to pay any further heed to the gryphon's

blatherings. 'Put me ashore on that rock,' he commanded, 'so I can release the girl from her chains.'

With a sigh, the gryphon deposited the dripping youngster at the captive damsel's feet.

Gustave took his first look at her from close at hand. Her hair fell to her hips in golden ringlets, her milk-white skin and regular features were as preternaturally flawless as—yes, as those of a classical marble statue. Her unclothed body accorded so perfectly with Gustave's ideal conception of beauty that . . . But he was compelled to lower his gaze, overwhelmed by a sensation that forbade him to feast his eyes on the helpless girl's form any longer.

Gustave had just fallen in love for the very first time, and that emotion, which is granted to every human being only once, was unlike any he had ever experienced before.

At last he ventured to look up again. There was such a strange expression in the girl's sea-blue eyes that he couldn't immediately interpret it. Gratitude? (She seemed to be struck dumb.) Timidity? (She seemed unable to look him in the eye.) Eternal love? (Her ecstatic gaze seemed focused on the far distant future.)

'I thought the boy was meant to wind up dead,' she said at length in a cold, sarcastic voice. She was, in fact, addressing the gryphon, for her eyes had really been focused on the mythical beast hovering in the background.

'What's the meaning of this idiotic business?' she went on. 'He's killed my pet dragon. Who's going to replace it? I've hung around here in the spray for hours on end. My skin has gone all soft, and I wouldn't be surprised if I'm suffering from sunburn.' She slipped out of her chains with ease and covered her nakedness with her flowing tresses.

'You'll receive compensation,' the gryphon told her in a coolly condescending tone. 'Events took an unforeseen turn. I can't help that, I'm just a servant of Death.'

'Aren't we all?' The girl gave a disdainful laugh. Without sparing Gustave another glance, she proceeded to clamber nimbly up the rocks.

Gustave's heart broke. It broke into two precisely equal parts, the one that belonged irrevocably to the lovely damsel, and the other that was all he had left. An icy void seemed to open up inside him. It was worse than any physical pain he had ever endured.

The gryphon glided down and rested one wing on Gustave's shoulder. 'I told you, didn't I?' it said. 'There are worse things in life than dragons. Falling in love, for instance.'

When the gryphon bore him away from the Island of Damsels in Distress, Gustave was in a condition resembling rigor mortis. White as a sheet and glassy-eyed, he sat astride the creature, heedless of the cold air rushing past, even though he had few clothes on and his hair was still wet with sea water.

'You'd welcome Death in your present state,' remarked the gryphon, which occasionally turned to give its passenger a look of concern and tried to cheer him up. If it hadn't been for the gryphon, Gustave would probably have sunk down on the damsel's rock, consumed with despair, and been devoured by the next dragon to come along. As it was, the creature had eventually convinced him that it would be smarter to climb aboard and let himself be conveyed to the scene of his next task. There he would be provided with fresh clothes and equipment and a suitable means of transportation.

The sea displayed scarcely a ripple as they sped across it to a peninsula not far away, which itself formed part of a largish land mass. Gustave could see from above that the peninsula was densely wooded, and that looming in the interior was a bleak mountain range. The gryphon glided down and landed on the very tip of the tongue of land. Gustave dismounted and listened apathetically to its instructions on his future movements.

'From here on, you can only proceed by land. Flying is impossible in this air space, and I'm not designed to travel on foot. You'll be wondering why on earth a forest reputed to be swarming with goblins and other horrific creatures could be less of a threat than the sky above it.'

Gustave did not pursue this point, so the gryphon went on, 'I'll tell you why: because that air space up there is full of appalling dangers! There are holes in the sky that are said to lead to other dimensions. The ethereal ocean above this territory is dominated by flying serpents and other malign creatures.'

'I can't see any,' said Gustave, unimpressed.

'But you can see the air quivering above the treetops?'

Gustave nodded. 'It's hot, that's all—heated by the perpetual sunshine.'

'Don't you believe it! Those are aeolian slicers. They're like glass—transparent and almost invisible, but sharp as cut-throat razors. You don't notice them until *after* they've reduced you to slices.'

Gustave was growing tired of the mythical beast's dissertation.

'You can rest here awhile,' it continued. 'Your new travelling companion is on the way with your equipment. He'll be here before long.' The gryphon rose into the air. 'As for your love-sickness,' it added, 'it'll pass. The more your first love hurts, the quicker you'll forget how wonderful it was. You won't find that much of a comfort at present, but you will, believe me.'

Gustave sank to the ground, stretched out in the long grass, heaved a deep sigh, and instantly fell asleep.

ustave was roused by a clatter of hoofs. He opened his eyes and sleepily raised his head. All he could make out at first was a wavering figure, a creature with four legs and a human torso. Another mythical creature? A centaur?

He blinked, and his vision cleared. A magnificent silver-grey horse came trotting out of the forest with a knight on its back. The latter, who was wearing a fearsome-looking suit of black armour and a helmet with the visor closed, carried a long wooden lance in his right hand and a spiked ball-and-chain in his left.

The knight levelled his lance and cleared his throat.

'Get ready for your last task!' he called to Gustave, who was laboriously scrambling to his feet. The voice was deep and metallic, as though the armour itself were speaking.

'What does he mean, my *last* task?' thought Gustave, bewildered. 'And why a knight?' No one had ever said anything about doing battle with a knight. He straightened up with an effort, brushing the earth and leaves off his arms and legs. It was only then that he remembered how scantily attired he was.

Gustave decided to clear the air by appealing to reason. The knight, who was doubtless his new travelling companion, had evidently been given the wrong instructions. Someone had definitely blundered. Either that, or the figure in black was playing a silly practical joke on him.

'Now look here,' Gustave began, but the pugnacious warrior had spurred his horse and was galloping towards him. The ball-and-chain whistled through the air as he whirled it around his head, dust and clumps of grass went flying, and the forest floor shook in time to the charger's hoofbeats.

Gustave tried to react as the situation warranted: he reached for his sword, but it wasn't there any more. It was embedded in the belly of a hapless dragon lying dead on the seabed.

'I'm a servant of Death!' bellowed the black knight, digging his spurs into the charger's flanks.

'That's no surprise,' Gustave muttered to himself as he desperately scanned his surroundings for somewhere to take cover.

The whistle of the ball-and-chain and the thunder of hoofs combined to create a kind of music that grew louder and more menacing as the horse bounded nearer. The knight himself emitted an awe-inspiring sound which had probably served him well in many a battle—a cross between a growl and a rising scream. Its effect was not lost on Gustave, who at last decided that discretion was the better part of valour. His intention was to sprint into the nearby forest, where a horse would find it hard to follow and the knight, in his heavy armour, would also have problems. But he couldn't move. His feet seemed to be rooted to the spot—he couldn't budge them even an inch.

Looking down, he saw that his ankles were trapped by two tendrils—no ordinary tendrils, however. Although they were of the same olive-green colour as the other plants around, they had tiny, elfin faces, dainty but athletic bodies, and muscular-looking hands and arms. Embedded in the ground from the waist down, they wore little hats consisting of upturned flower cups.

'Don't run away!' one of them called in a piping voice. 'Stand your ground!'

'Yes!' snarled the other. 'Abandon yourself to your fate!'

'*The forest of evil spirits,*' Gustave thought suddenly, '*—I must be in the midst of it already!*'

He strove to free himself, but the stubborn elves hung on tight.

'At last there's going to be some action around here!' the first one crowed delightedly.

'Yes, if you think we're going to let you get away, you're wrong!' said the other. 'We want to see the colour of your blood!'

Gustave redirected his attention to the knight, who by now was only a few lengths away. His metallic war cry had risen to a shriek, and foam was flying from the horse's muzzle.

It seemed to Gustave that his only option was to accept the inevitable. He sank to his knees, shielding his head with his hands, and watched the galloping knight bear down on him.

He resigned himself to the following sequence of events: (a) the lance would transfix his chest with a horrid noise; (b) horse and rider would come crashing down on him, breaking every bone in his body; and (c) the black knight could then, if he chose to, knock his head off his shoulders with the ball-and-chain. This was a thoroughly realistic assessment of his immediate future—at least for as long as these obnoxious elves continued to cling to his feet, and they showed no signs of letting go.

'You're dead!' yelled one.

'Now you can surrender your soul!' laughed the other.

What actually happened, however, was that the charging horse seemed suddenly to slow down. To be more precise, *every* movement made by the horse and its rider seemed to become more protracted, as if someone had applied the brakes to time itself.

The black knight's voice became unnaturally deep, like the lowest note of a tuba. His mailed left fist, which was swinging the ball-and-chain, detached itself from his arm and, propelled through the air by the weapon's momentum, flew off into the forest. The cast-iron ball embedded its spikes in the trunk of a birch tree, the mailed fist swung ponderously to and fro on the end of the rattling chain. Gustave stared in astonishment as the knight's right arm fell off, leaving a hole through which he could see that the armour was empty. The left leg broke loose, keeled over sideways, and was dragged along by the stirrup, the remains of the left arm went flying, as did the other leg. The helmet, which also fell off, was as empty as everything else. Then the rest of the armour crashed to the ground. All that was left was the horse, which threw back its head and drove its hoofs into the ground. Great clods of earth went flying past Gustave's ears as the animal skidded to a halt only inches short of him.

That was when he woke up. He was still lying where he had sunk to the ground after the gryphon had taken its leave. Standing beside him was a nag that bore not the slightest resemblance to the proud warhorse of his nightmare. Considerably leaner and far less handsome, it was pawing the ground, snorting, and nervously frisking to and fro.

'Good morning,' it said.

Although Gustave was surprised to encounter a horse that could speak, another beast with the power of speech was no big deal in view of recent developments, so he merely returned its salutation.

'Good morning,' he said sleepily.

'My name is Pancho,' the horse said, '—Pancho Sansa.'

'Pancho Sansa?' thought Gustave. 'What a silly name, and why does it sound so familiar?' Courtesy seemed to prescribe that he introduce himself likewise.

'My name is Gustave—'

'—Doré,' the horse cut in. 'Yes, I know. I'm your next travelling companion. I'm afraid I lost your new suit of armour in the forest back there. The undergrowth was so dense, it knocked the stuff off my back. I'll show you where the pieces are lying. Then you can put on your ironmongery and we'll go and give a few of these evil spirits what for, agreed?'

A herd of graceful deer fled, startled by the intrusive sound of Pancho's hoofs as he trotted across a verdant meadow with Gustave on his back. Gustave was in full armour once more. His accoutrements weren't black and fearsome-looking, like those of the knight in his dream, but made of fine chased silver like the ones he had worn before.

A flock of birds with exotic plumage took wing, twittering indignantly, and disappeared into the tangle of branches and creepers. Spiders' webs floated through the air, forming gossamer-fine rope ladders up which the little light that remained was ascending into the evening sky. Glow-worms—or were they will-o'-the-wisps?—began to dance and fill the air with multicoloured squiggles.

'This must be the enchanted forest,' said Gustave.

'Know what forests give me?' asked Pancho. 'The creeps! Yessir, I'm more of a prairie type. Wide-open spaces, fields, meadows, deserts—even roads, provided they're long and straight. Forests are the bitter end. Mountains are bad enough, but forests—'

'Ssh,' said Gustave. 'What was that?'

Pancho gave a snort of alarm. 'What was what?'

'Oh, nothing,' muttered Gustave. 'I thought I heard something, that's all.'

Faint singing pervaded the air of the forest, mingled with crackling, rustling noises. Now and then, acorns and twigs landed on Gustave's helmet as if someone had deliberately chucked them at him.

'You're right,' whispered Pancho, 'this forest is bewitched.'

It seemed to Gustave that they had for some time been riding along the bed of a long-dried-up river. The ground was littered with big, smooth pebbles, banks of earth the height of a man towered on either side, thick with grass and bushesb, and the winding track described a series of sharp bends. The trees became steadily denser. Grotesquely stunted oaks stood cheek by jowl, intertwining their mighty branches and shutting out the evening sunlight. Before long the two travellers were overarched by an impenetrable canopy of foliage.

They trotted along with a sense of foreboding until, as they rounded yet another bend in the river bed, an unforeseen and startling sight met their eyes. Ahead of them, seated beneath an immense oak tree, was an old woman.

Although the roots writhing out of the ground around her looked as if they might envelop the frail old crone at any moment and drag her down into some subterranean, elfin realm, she seemed to have no fear of the enchanted forest.

She had folded her hands on her lap and was staring grimly into space. What with her sunken cheeks, the little crown on her head, and her voluminous black robe, she looked like a deposed monarch who had been banished to the depths of the forest to await death by starvation. Above her, perched on a root and imitating her grim expression, sat an owl.

Gustave and Pancho rode very, very slowly past the old lady so as not to startle her, but she took no notice of either of them, just looked straight through them as if gazing into another dismal dimension.

They were just about to round the next bend and lose sight of this strange apparition when Gustave reined in.

'What's the matter?' whispered Pancho. 'Let's ride on. The poor old biddy's cracked. They're nothing but trouble, people like that.'

'I don't know,' Gustave whispered back. 'She looks *familiar* to me, somehow.'

He tugged at the bridle, wheeled Pancho round, and rode back.

'Allow me to introduce myself,' he said. 'I'm Gustave Doré.'

'Eh?' The old woman was visibly taken aback by this courteous approach. Her vacant expression was replaced by one of dismay. She started to gesticulate, only to stop short in mid movement.

'Doré,' Gustave repeated politely in a somewhat louder voice. 'Gustave Doré.'

'Hell's bells!' the old woman blurted out.

'Excuse me?'

'Gustave Doré . . . ' she said, as if to herself. 'You, of all people!'

She cackled insanely, muttered something that sounded like 'Incredible!' and 'That's all I needed!' and brushed some invisible crumbs off her robe. Then she seemed to quieten. 'What are *you* doing here?' she asked curtly, looking straight at Gustave.

To his ears, the question sounded as if it had been asked by someone he'd known for a considerable time and had now re-encountered in an exotic, outlandish place. It also sounded as if that someone was anything but pleased to have renewed their acquaintance.

Closer examination convinced him that he didn't know the old woman at all—indeed, familiar though she still seemed, he was sure he'd never seen her before. Despite the bewildering nature of the situation, he tried to answer her question as truthfully as possible.

'I'm on my way to perform a task for Death. Several tasks, in fact. It's a complicated business. That's why I have to cross this forest. Do you know it well?'

The old lady laughed rather too loudly—almost hysterically, it seemed to Gustave.

'Me? This forest? Do I know it well?' She cackled again, so violently that she choked and had a coughing fit. Then, fixing Gustave with an expression which, though grave and stern, was somewhat less unfriendly than before, she asked, 'So you'd like to know what route to take?'

Gustave thought for a moment. 'It might be helpful,' he replied.

'Aren't you getting to be of an age when you ought to make such decisions yourself?'

Gustave was taken aback. He hadn't been prepared for such a searching question.

'Just keep going, boy! I don't know you and you don't know me. You only think you know me. Be off with you!'

Gustave was about to ride on, chastened by the black–clad figure's brusque manner, when her last remark brought him up short. 'How did you know you seem familiar to me?' he asked. 'I never said anything about it.'

The old woman avoided his eye and bit her lip. 'Damnation!' she muttered.

'Who are you?' asked Gustave. 'What are you doing here, all alone in this deep, dark forest?'

'I, er . . . I'm a forest witch. An *evil* forest witch!' croaked the old woman, but she didn't sound too convincing. Her eyes roamed uncertainly to and fro, and she fidgeted with her robe in embarrassment. In Gustave's estimation, an evil forest witch would have been a bit more self-assured.

'I'm an evil forest witch in a good mood!' the old crone added quickly. 'Better take advantage of the fact and get going before I transform you into, er, stinging nettles, or something of the kind.' She opened her eyes wide and waggled her bony fingers in the air.

'Come on, let's go,' Pancho called impatiently. 'We're not wanted here.'

'How is it I don't believe you?' Gustave asked as politely and amiably as he could. 'How come I get the feeling I know you, although I've never seen you before? Can you explain that?'

The old woman bowed her head and fidgeted with her robe some more. 'Yes, I can,' she said, and it seemed to Gustave that she was blushing.

'Oh, really?'

'Yes, I can . . . ' The old woman lifted her head and looked him in the eye. 'I'll have to go back a bit, but you'll understand in the end.' The note of uncertainty had left her voice, and she seemed to be getting ready to tell the truth. She raised her hands and spread her wizened fingers.

'Very well, picture the following: a large department store—one of those modern places that exist in big cities nowadays. You're employed at the information desk. You know, you're one of those nice people at the counter on the ground floor who tell you where to find the menswear department.'

Gustave nodded, Pancho snorted contemptuously.

'You've had the job for a long time, so you know the store like the back of your hand, but it's recently been undergoing alterations.

Departments keep being transferred to different floors, builders are at work everywhere, walls are being demolished and new ones erected. You don't feel as thoroughly at home there as you used to. Are you with me so far?'

'Yes,' said Gustave, 'I think so.'

'Good,' said the old woman. 'Now, imagine you suddenly need to go to the *men's room*!'

'To the men's room?' Gustave repeated uncomprehendingly.

'Let's get out of here,' Pancho whispered.

'Ssh!' Gustave hissed.

'So you set off,' pursued the old woman. 'Of course you know the way to the toilets—you've directed people there a thousand times—but now you find your way barred by a maze of walls that weren't there before. Whole departments have been uprooted, and you have to change floors several times. All at once it dawns on you: *You don't know where the toilets are.*'

Gustave tried to picture the situation. There was something amusing about it, but also something alarming.

'Now comes the worst part: just then, the owner of the store— *your boss!*—comes up to you and asks you *the way to the toilets.*'

The old woman paused and gave Gustave a searching stare. 'You see? We're in just the same situation here and now.'

'Oo-hoo!' cried the owl.

Although Gustave held the old woman's gaze, he couldn't think what she was getting at. Pancho made some impatient noises.

'Don't you understand?' the old woman blurted out. 'I'm your *dream princess!*'

'You're a dream princess?' said Gustave, still politely. Pancho seemed to be right: the poor old thing was deranged. He searched around for some suitable way of bringing the conversation to an end.

'Not only that: I'm *your own personal dream princess!*'

Gustave had a rather different conception of his own personal dream princess. He pictured her as golden-haired and considerably younger—just like the damsel he'd 'rescued' from the dragon, to be precise.

He felt an icy little stab in the chest.

The old woman sighed. 'Listen, my boy. Everyone has someone to guide them through their dreams. Men have a dream princess, women a dream prince. That's what we're called—I didn't invent the term myself. Personally, I think it's a pompous and inappropriate job description. I'd prefer *dream consultant.*'

She cleared her throat.

'That's why I seem so familiar to you. You've often come across me, but always in a different guise. Those are the rules: a different guise for every dream. This time it's *this* idiotic get-up.' She gave her heavy robe a disapproving tweak and tapped her little crown.

'Do you remember that dream where you climbed a tree made of meat with a red raven perched on top? I was the raven.'

Gustave seldom if ever remembered a dream, and he certainly had no recollection of one with a red raven in it. 'Just a minute,' he said. 'Are you telling me that this is all a dream? The forest, you yourself, my horse—all just a dream?'

'Ridiculous!' Pancho snorted and stamped his left hoof impatiently.

The old woman groaned.

'You asked me a question and I answered it. I advised you to ride on, but you stayed. I lied to you, but you wanted the truth. I even pretended to be a witch. What else do you want me to do?'

'I can't believe it,' said Gustave. 'Everything seems so . . . well, real.'

'A talking horse? An enchanted forest? An old woman who tells you she's a dream princess? You call that *real*?' The old woman, who couldn't help laughing, choked and had another coughing fit.

'But if none of this is real,' Gustave objected, 'then *you* don't exist either.'

The old woman's face suddenly stiffened again.

'Believe me, my boy,' she said gravely, 'that's a problem I've been debating for a very long time—whenever I've a spare moment, in fact.'

Gustave tried to argue logically.

'If you're my very own dream princess—or dream consultant, whichever—what are you doing here in the middle of the forest?'

'That's the embarrassing part: I've *lost my way*. I don't know where the toilets are!' The old woman gave a bitter laugh. 'I've no idea what's gone wrong with your dreams of late, but they've definitely been getting wilder. Perhaps it's got something to do with your age. You'll soon be leaving childhood behind.'

'I haven't been a child for ages!' Gustave protested with a scowl. 'I'm twelve already!'

'Yes, yes,' the dream princess said dismissively, 'but don't be *too* keen to grow up.' She eyed her wrinkled hands with distaste.

'What has *my* age got to do with *you* losing your way?' Gustave asked sharply.

'How should I know? I'm merely voicing conjectures. I'm only a dream consultant, after all. What's more, I'm doing the job for the first time.' The old woman grunted. 'Earlier on you used to dream about rabbits, about your parents, and building bricks, and the red ball you were so fond of playing with, and the ducks in the park. But lately—good heavens! Dragons! Winged monsters? Talking jellyfish! Naked girls! No wonder the likes of me can't find my way around your dreams any more.'

Gustave blushed. How did she know about his adventures on the Island of Damsels in Distress? Their conversation was becoming more and more bewildering.

'Pin your ears back,' said the dream consultant, 'and I'll give you a rundown on the way dreams work—as far as my information goes, that is. A short course in dreamology for beginners, right?'

Gustave nodded.

'You must simply think of the dream-world as another country, and when you dream you're going on a journey through that country. You're travelling, even though you're lying in bed without budging from the spot. Dreams are the most fantastic free rides imaginable. We really ought to sell tickets for them.'

'Could you cut the cackle a bit?' Pancho grumbled. 'We've got things to do before the day's out.'

The old woman ignored him. 'The dream-world is an unpredictable place,' she went on, '—the most lawless place in the entire universe. A jungle composed of time, space and providence, of hindsight and foresight, of fears and desires, all jumbled up together.' She knotted her fingers into a dense latticework.

'A country, a jungle, a department store,' thought Gustave. 'Whatever next?'

'So it's helpful if there's someone around to give you an occasional tip, an item of information, a covert hint. That's what we dream princesses are there for.'

'I see,' said Gustave.

'No, you don't!' snapped the old woman. 'Listen carefully! I can assume the guise of an articulate apple or a chicken made of cheese. Remember the cheese chicken that advised you to cough three times?'

'No,' said Gustave.

'Never mind. Anyway, it was a prime example of professional dream consultancy. The dream was a nightmare, and you were on the point of drowning in a pool of rice pudding when I turned up as the chicken made of cheese and advised you to cough three times. You coughed in your sleep, and that woke you up.'

'I don't remember.'

'That's the dark shadow that looms over our endeavours: the shadow of oblivion.' The old woman heaved a sigh. 'We dream consultants have learned to get by without any pats on the back.'

'So do most people,' Gustave retorted, rather proud of having come up with such a precocious remark.

'Now, now, young man, you've no cause to make fun of our work. Dream consultancy is a hard, unrewarding job, and one that often seems pointless. Besides, nobody can be sure the same fate won't befall them. You could become one yourself some day.'

'Me, a dream princess?'

Pancho whinnied with laughter.

'Not a princess, of course: a dream *prince*.'

'How come?'

'Basically, anyone can work in dream consultancy as long as he fulfils certain conditions. First you've got to *die*. That's the most important qualification for the job.'

'Just a minute!' Gustave exclaimed. 'Does that mean you're dead?'

'Dead as a doornail, otherwise we wouldn't be talking together now. I died . . . let's see . . . two hundred and seventy-three years ago. We're related, by the way. I'm your great-great-great-grandmother—on your father's side.'

Gustave opened his mouth to speak, but the old woman got in first.

'I died at the age of ninety-nine, after a long and fulfilled life. That's the second basic precondition for a career in dream consultancy: you must have a *fulfilled* life behind you. People with unsatisfying lives tend to be unstable characters, which renders them unfitted for our profession.'

Gustave nodded.

'Enjoy a life of fulfilment and then switch to dream consultancy. That's the only way to escape Death and his soul-coffins.'

'You know about the soul-coffins?'

The old woman grinned.

'*No sun, no life; no life, no souls; no souls, no sun—that's the everlasting cycle of the univ* . . .' She clapped a hand over her mouth in mock horror. 'Whoops! I almost gave away one of the great mysteries of the universe!' She laughed.

'How can you tell whether someone has led a fulfilled life?' asked Gustave. He had never taken part in such an absurd conversation, but he was beginning to enjoy it.

'Hard to say. You can't tell until the end. It's got nothing to do with longevity or success or satisfaction or the like. You look back on your life and see it lying ahead of you—or behind you, as the case may be.'

She giggled.

'I can't tell you *what* indicates whether a life was fulfilled or not, only that it's possible to see it. Even godforsaken Death can see it. Then he takes his soul-coffin, the stupid bag of bones, and pushes off.'

Pancho cleared his throat. 'Are you going to be much longer, the pair of you? I mean, we've still got a few tasks to perform, and—'

'True,' said Gustave. The conversation had become more interesting than he'd originally thought, and he would have liked to question the old lady further, because he still couldn't decide whether she was really deranged or simply teasing him in a subtle way. But Pancho was right, they had more important things to do.

'We must ride on.'

'I know,' said the old woman.

'One last question,' Gustave called over his shoulder when they were trotting along the dried-up river bed once more. 'If you really have lost your way in my dreams, how will you manage to get out again?'

The old lady laughed, and he saw for the first time that all her teeth were of glittering gold.

'I'll do like the information desk in the department store: I'll wait until closing time.'

'How do you mean?'

'I'll wait till you wake up,' she said.

She smoothed her robe down, adjusted her crown, and reassumed her blank expression. The owl emitted a few scornful cries, but by that time Gustave and Pancho were beyond the next bend and well out of sight.

'If you ask me,' said Pancho, as they rode on along the dried-up river bed with a dense canopy of branches over-head, 'the old dear had a screw loose. Did you understand all that stuff about the rabbit and the ducks?'

'Nobody *did* ask you,' Gustave retorted, but he continued to ponder the question. No, to be honest, the bit about the rabbit and the ducks had defeated him too.

'We ought to concentrate on your tasks now,' said Pancho. 'I'm as anxious to get out of this godforsaken forest as you are.'

'We have to make ourselves conspicuous,' Gustave remembered.

'Meaning what?'

'We have to draw attention to ourselves in the Forest of Evil Spirits—that's part of the task.'

'In that case,' said the horse, 'I suggest we sing. Sensitive souls find music considerably more of a pain than is generally supposed. Can you sing?'

'Yes,' replied Gustave, who was, in fact, quite musical. 'I can sing pretty well.'

'That's bad,' Pancho snickered. 'It'd be better if you couldn't. Musical singing isn't as noticeable as unmusical singing. You're in luck, though: *I* can't sing for toffee, so I'll take over that part of the task.' He cleared his throat. 'Do you know *The Song of the Horse that Ate Too Much Ghost-Grass*?'

'Ghost-grass?'

'Yes, a nasty weed. I ate some myself on one occasion, but that's another story. Just listen. Normally it's neighed, being a horse song, but I'll do my best to translate it into your inadequate language.'

Having snorted a couple of times, the horse proceeded to belt out its ballad in an unmelodious baritone:

Alas, I've eaten of the herb
whose roots lie in the underworld,
and now, with senses all aflame,
the magic spell I must declaim:
'Ye evil sprites that fly and crawl,
obey my summons, one and all.
Dreams and reality unite!
Night turn to day, and day to night!'
Light and shade, together blending,
shroud my eyes in mists unending,
and behold, from out the gloom,
soulless, restless spirits loom.
Loud their mocking cries resound
as they boldly prance around.
See, the mists grow thicker yet,
and by nightmares I'm beset.
While I stand there all alone,
incorporeal shadows moan,
long-legged spiders do their work,
weaving webs in which to lurk,
gargoyle faces mop and mow
with rolling eyes and skulls that glow,
and mouths emitting frightful screams
that will forever haunt my dreams.
Enough of this! Back to your lair:

the underworld. It isn't fair
of you to plague me thus, so go!
'Twas but a joke of mine, you know.
Shoo! Go away! Well, are you deaf?
Be off with you, I've had enough.
I ate some ghost-grass, nothing more,
so now that's it: you know the score.
Ghost-grass is just a friendly weed
that blows your mind—it's what you need
to banish all your cares and woe.
Hey, what's all this? Please let me go!
Stop tugging at my hoofs like that!
Help, help! I'm sinking!

'That last line didn't rhyme *or* scan,' Gustave said irritably. Pancho's frightful doggerel had been getting on his nerves. What was more, the horse had simply come to a halt without a by-your-leave.

'That wasn't part of the song! I really *am* sinking!'

Pancho's voice was panic-stricken, and Gustave could detect some curious crackling, sucking sounds coming from beneath him. He looked down at the horse's legs. All four of them were buried up to their fetlocks in spongy moss.

'The ground must be rather soft here,' said Gustave. 'We'd better—'

'But something's tugging at me!' cried Pancho. 'I'm being dragged down!'

There was a sudden jerk that nearly pitched Gustave out of the saddle, and Pancho sank up to his hocks in the forest floor. Gustave jumped off, keeping hold of the reins. He was surprised to find that *his* feet didn't sink into the moss at all. The carpet of vegetation beneath him was perfectly firm and dry, but Pancho, as if he'd strayed on to an expanse of quicksand, was sinking deeper and deeper.

'What's going on here?' Gustave exclaimed.

'How should I know?' Pancho's voice broke. 'Get me out of here! Please!' There was another jerk, and he sank in up to his belly.

'Do something! Come on, quick!' Big bubbles of foam had formed around Pancho's muzzle, and his eyes were rolling in panic. Gustave wrenched at the reins and the horse tried to kick itself free, but there was another brutal tug from below. All that now protruded from the moss were Pancho's head and neck.

'Do something, can't you? Dig me out!' he whinnied in despair. Gustave knelt down and tried to scrape the moss away from his neck, but it was hard and deep-rooted. All he managed to dislodge were a few dry tufts.

'Swallowed up by the ground,' called Pancho. 'What a ridiculous way to go! It serves me right! Can you forgive me, at least?'

'Forgive you? What for?' demanded Gustave, desperately tugging at the reins again.

'My only job was to turn you over to the evil spirits. You won't be able to perform your task without being devoured by them.'

'What!'

'It's all a plot hatched by Death! No one has ever succeeded in escaping from the Forest of Evil Spirits. I never dreamt it would get me too. Please forgive me!' Pancho's big eyes filled with tears.

With a final jerk, his head disappeared and the reins were torn from Gustave's hands. The ground closed over Pancho with a lip-smacking sound: he had vanished without a trace.

Gustave got to his feet and stood there swaying, incapable of thinking clearly. He was utterly dazed by what had happened.

'Pancho?' he said stupidly.

The trees rustled as if their branches were stirring in the wind. The whispers and giggles Gustave had heard before began again, sounding louder and more alarming than ever.

The forest seemed to come alive. Branches lashed around, leaves went scudding through the air, treetops shook, bark crunched against bark. In the twinkling of an eye, Gustave found himself hemmed in by a formidable horde of forest demons of the most multifarious kinds. He was surrounded on all sides by lizard-tailed dwarfs, horned owls, beaked insects, and other bizarre apparitions. Creatures of darkness in every conceivable form came crowding towards him out of the forest's shadowy depths.

He froze and drew his sword, but hesitated to raise it and adopt a warlike pose.

Hanging head down from a branch above him was a batlike creature with an almost human face. 'Hey, you!' it said angrily. 'How did you have the nerve to sing such an impudent song in our forest?'

Gustave felt convinced that, under the circumstances, sticking to the truth would be the best policy.

'It wasn't me singing, it was my horse.'

'What horse?' the winged creature demanded spitefully.

'You know the one I mean,' said Gustave, trying to make a courteous but far from timid impression. 'I do admit, however, that I was deliberately trying to attract your attention. I made a wager with Death,' he went on, with only a slight tremor in his voice. 'One of my tasks is to behave in a conspicuous way.'

'Well, young man,' hissed the batlike creature, 'you've succeeded. You now have our undivided attention.'

'A wager with Death!' sneered a hideous dwarf mounted on an even more hideous pig. 'What's this, emotional blackmail? We all have to die some time.'

'Quite so!' exclaimed a one-legged bird with insect's antennae. 'We ought to hang him upside down from a copper beech and nibble his liver.'

'You mean you also have to die?' Gustave was bold enough to interject.

'Of course we do,' called a gnome with a child's face. He spread his arms and laughed. 'Everyone has to.'

'But you're spirits—creatures that dwell in limbo. I've never heard it said that goblins have to die.'

This threw the weird gathering into confusion. They all grunted and whispered together excitedly.

'When was the last time,' Gustave demanded, somewhat more firmly, 'that one of you departed this life?'

'Er . . .' said the one-legged bird.

'Mm . . .' added an owl in the background.

'Well . . .' conceded a beaked gnome seated astride an emu. 'I can't recall the last time someone died, I must admit.'

'Personally,' came a croak from a dark hole in a tree trunk, 'I can't remember anyone dying at all.'

'I've never attended a funeral,' murmured a frog standing on its hind legs.

'What's a funeral?' asked someone right at the back.

'I've got a great-grandmother who's four hundred and fifty years old,' mused a monstrous grasshopper, thoughtfully rubbing its stork's beak, 'and she herself has a grandmother who's still surprisingly chipper.'

A spiderlike creature the size of a loaf of bread had crawled up to Gustave from behind and was scratching his armour insistently with its forelegs.

'Are you suggesting,' it whispered in a reedy, otherworldly voice, 'that we're immortal?'

Gustave was beginning to realise that a self-assured manner was his best hope of dealing with this sinister crew. 'Well,' he said loudly and firmly, 'none of you has ever died yet, as you yourselves have noticed, even though some of you are over four hundred years old.'

'Seven hundred!' called an owl.

'Nine hundred!' something indefinable croaked proudly.

'Two thousand five hundred, in round figures,' bragged a lizard with umpteen feet and a goblin's head.

'All right,' Gustave continued, 'over *two thousand five hundred* years old. That strikes me as pretty good evidence of immortality. At the very least, it gives grounds for, er, optimistic speculation.'

The eerie band lapsed into pensive silence for a while. The hush was finally broken by the one-legged bird.

'That would be wonderful,' it said. 'I mean, I could stop worrying about these periodic pains in my left wing. If we aren't destined to die, it's unlikely that I'll suffer a fatal heart attack or—'

'It would brighten our whole existence,' the hideous hog broke in. 'We could dismiss all thoughts of death. That would mean a hundred per cent improvement in our quality of life.'

'It would spell the end of all the confounded pessimism in this forest,' predicted the dwarf on its back.

'This is splendid!' exclaimed the owl. 'We're immortal!'

'Hurrah!'

'Immortal!'

The forest rang with jubilant cries, whistles and laughter. The creatures embraced, slapped each other's backs and humps, shed tears of joy. Gustave stood idly by until the commotion subsided.

'Good!' cried the one-legged bird, hopping over to Gustave and resting one wing on his shoulder. 'This nice young man entered our forest in order to help us lead lives free from fear. Hip-hip-hip!'

'Hurray! Hurray! Hurray!' cheered the spirits.

Gustave began to relax.

'And now,' the bird went on gaily, 'let's hang him upside down from the copper beech and devour his liver!'

Gustave recoiled a step and raised the sword above his head. 'So I'm in for a fight after all,' he thought.

The one-legged bird uttered a malevolent titter. The pig grunted avidly as though guzzling a truffle. The other creatures, too, emitted strangely rhythmical sounds which Gustave could only interpret as their own peculiar form of laughter.

'Forgive me!' croaked the bird, gasping for breath. 'Forgive my inability to refrain from cracking that rather distasteful joke. Of course we won't devour your liver!'

Gustave lowered his sword.

'We'd never do *that*. Human livers are full of poisons. Naturally, we won't devour anything but your *brain*!'

The clearing rang with more hysterical laughter. Gustave took up his defensive stance once more.

'Hey, come on now!' the bird exclaimed between guffaws. 'Put that silly sword away and relax! Make a few allowances for our demonic sense of humour! We're not going to eat you. You're invited to a party. Be our guest!'

And, as though at a given signal, all the horrific creatures proceeded to dance round Gustave. Singing weird songs, they drew their reluctant guest ever deeper into the darkness of the forest.

It was—at least from Gustave's point of view—a quite extra-ordinary party. The way in which the forest demons amused themselves differed entirely from any form of jollity he had ever come across. Their grotesque jig ended in a small clearing. Here the piglike creatures began to root in the soft forest floor and toss truffles around, grunting, while the birdlike creatures tore each other's feathers out with their beaks and the goblins hammered their heads against tree trunks, bellowing imprecations until their noses bled.

A copper cauldron filled with seething wine-red liquid was suspended over a blue fire. Everyone danced around this, throwing in herbs and stinging nettles, mushrooms and truffles. The brew gave off gurgling bubbles, some of which detached themselves from the surface and floated up to the canopy of foliage overhead, where they disappeared. Several of the demons beat hollow trees or thick roots with branches and stones, creating a throbbing rhythm to which the others moved convulsively.

The owls joined in, hooting in deep bass voices, and eerie singing issued from knotholes in the trees. The scene was provided with ever-changing illumination by multicoloured will-o'-the-wisps that meandered drunkenly through the air, lighting up and going out in time to the music. A duck-footed gnome with a face like an ecstatic pig cavorted past, hitting himself on the head with a stone. Heavy with the scent of smouldering herbs, swathes of dense green smoke drifted among the revellers. It made Gustave dizzy just to watch.

'Here, have some!' called a hunchbacked frog, holding out a beaker filled with the foaming red brew. Gustave thanked him politely and took a reluctant sip. It didn't taste of much—a hint of iron and tomatoes, perhaps—but it instantly went to his head.

'Mm, delicious,' he lied, and downed half the contents of the beaker. His tongue seemed to absorb the liquid like a sponge and convey it straight to his brain. The one-legged bird that had done most of the talking hopped over to him and stood there, swaying.

'So you've passed your test with flying colours,' the feathered gnome said approvingly. 'You've made yourself conspicuous in a forest full of spirits *and you're still alive*! No one has ever managed that before. Congratulations!' It raised a beaker of the red brew with its right wing and toasted Gustave, who took another big swig for courtesy's sake.

'Thanks,' he said, belching faintly. 'It was easy enough, though.'

'What's your next test?' the bird enquired, slurring the words. Gustave could tell from the creature's unfocused eyes and huge, dilated pupils that it was already very drunk. 'A ride on a comet, or something of that order?'

'No,' Gustave replied, 'I have to guess the names of six giants.' He couldn't help laughing, not only because the task sounded so absurd, but because the red beverage was inducing such a state of hilarity that almost everything seemed laughable to him, even the prospect of tackling six giants.

'You're a courageous young man,' burbled the bird. 'Anyone making for the Plain of the Terrible Titans has to pass through the Valley of the Monsters. Your sword'll come in handy. Know how to use the thing?'

'I killed a dragon with it.'

'I take my hat off to you,' the bird exclaimed, and turned to its companions. 'Did you hear that?' it squawked above the din. 'This youngster here has killed a genuine dragon.'

But the other forest demons, who were growing more and more frenzied, had lost interest in them. They pranced around, twitching and bellowing, waved their arms in the air, or curled up on the ground, groaning, and tore out tufts of grass. Oddly enough, Gustave felt a strong temptation to follow their example.

'A dragon, eh?' the one-legged bird went on. It draped a long wing round Gustave's shoulders and gazed deep into his eyes. 'Did you also see some, er . . . naked damsels?'

Gustave felt a cold stab in the heart.

'Yes,' he replied, 'I did.'

'Whee . . .' the bird trilled admiringly. It rolled its bloodshot eyes and shook its wing as if to convey that it had burnt it on something hot.

'But tell me,' said Gustave, to change the subject, 'what was all that about the Valley of the Monsters and the Plain of the Terrible Titans? It sounds as if you know how to get there.'

'You're already on the way!' The bird grinned and raised its beaker again.

'What do you mean?' Gustave tried to say, but his tongue had almost gone on strike. The bird doubled, trebled and quadrupled under his bleary gaze, assuming a variety of colours as it did so: first pink, then red, then purple.

'I meant what I said: *You're already on the way!*' croaked the bird's metallic voice. A rattling sound made itself heard. Gustave wondered why it sounded familiar. Of course! It was the sound of carriage wheels turning briskly, mingled with the crunch of gravel and the thud of baggage landing on the roof.

Baggage? On what sort of roof? Here in the forest? There! A trumpet! No, a huntsman's horn. More like it, but still wrong. Of course, it was a ship's foghorn! Fog? A ship? In the Forest of Evil Spirits? Was he dreaming? Then came a whistling sound. No, that was no bird, it was a stationmaster's whistle.

'Can you hear it too?' asked Gustave, afraid he might be losing his mind. His speech, too, was slurred.

The bird grinned again.

'No, but I know what you mean. It's the *Wanderlust Wine* that does it—look.' The bird held out its beaker, and Gustave felt as if he were gazing into a whirlpool of blood. Contrary to every law of nature, the dark red liquid was rotating in a foaming spiral, the very sight of which gave him vertigo.

'Wanderlust Wine?' he repeated.

'Yes,' the bird confided in an undertone. 'Life is a journey! Perilous, unpredictable and full of surprises, even if you spend it sitting in an armchair without ever budging from the spot.' The creature emitted a hoarse laugh. 'Yes, that's Wanderlust Wine for you,' it croaked. 'Specially brewed for you at Death's expense.'

'What!' Gustave cried. 'You mean you're servants of Death?'

The bird raised its beaker in salute. A few other forest demons followed suit. 'Aren't we all?' they chorused.

'But you're immortal, surely?' said Gustave.

'So what?' The bird grinned. 'There's no reason why we shouldn't do Death an occasional favour.'

Gustave felt dizzy again. Yellow and green will-o'-the-wisps darted around in front of his nose, tying themselves in such intricate knots that they made him squint. He shut his eyes and instantly felt better. Whoops! He experienced a jolt of the kind you feel on board a train as it pulls out of the station.

A cool breeze fanned his face, as if he were sitting on the coachman's seat of a speeding carriage-and-four. Next he was engulfed by the metallic rumble and roar of a locomotive thundering through a tunnel at full steam ahead. Then, suddenly, he seemed to be on the deck of a ship with wind swirling about him and canvas flapping.

He still didn't dare to open his eyes; on the contrary, he kept them tightly shut and relied on his other senses. It was as though the odours of exotic lands were wafting past his nostrils: cinnamon, nutmeg, coriander, lemon grass, the scents of the jungle, the fragrance of orchids. He heard people speaking in different tongues, oriental music, high-pitched, singsong voices, a glockenspiel, the rhythmical thudding of drums, hands clapping, feet pounding, and—once more—wheels rattling over cobblestones, locomotives hissing, sailcloth flapping, hoofs clattering.

He opened his eyes at last.

The forest had vanished, and with it the inebriated bird and its frightful companions. Gustave was in the midst of a raging inferno of light and darkness. Day followed night at one-second intervals, as if the earth were rotating a thousand times faster than usual. Unfolding beneath him at breakneck speed were asphalted high-ways, broad avenues, sandy tracks, narrow paths. Mountains and whole landscapes sped past—steppes, deserts, rippling cornfields—as if some immense hand were towing him round the planet upside down. Clouds gathered and dispersed at an incredible rate. Time seemed to stand still inside Gustave while racing past him more wildly than ever. He felt sick and giddy. Unable to endure such a wealth of visual impressions, he shut his eyes again. A sudden jolt, a squeal of metal on metal, someone said 'Whoa!', a siren blared, anchor chains rattled, and he came to an abrupt halt. Total silence fell.

ustave opened his eyes. He was on a rocky eminence overlooking a gloomy valley. Grey weeds sprouted among the barren stones, blighted trees brooded sadly on granite crags, thick layers of cloud overarched the entire landscape like a shroud. The sun had almost set, and shadows were beginning to steal across the valley.

'My goodness,' Gustave exclaimed. 'Amazing, what Wanderlust Wine does to you!' He emitted an involuntary burp.

'I *beg* your pardon!' said a voice from beneath him.

Looking down, he found that he was sitting astride Pancho Sansa, his talking horse. 'How did *you* get here?' he asked in amazement.

'"How did *you* get here?"' Pancho mimicked resentfully. 'Is that all you can think of to say? How about: "Lord, am I glad you're still alive!" or "How on earth did you manage to extricate yourself?" or something of the kind? Pah!' He gave an offended snort.

Gustave felt ashamed. Of course he was genuinely glad to see Pancho unscathed after that frightful episode in the forest. He groped for the right words.

'Lord, am I glad you're still alive!' he said eventually and rather unoriginally. 'How on earth did you manage to extricate yourself?' He forced a smile and gave the horse's neck a clumsy pat.

'Stop that!' Still disgruntled, Pancho shook his hand off.

'Now look here!' said Gustave. 'If anyone's entitled to play the injured party, I reckon it's me. You lured me into the forest and abandoned me to those evil spirits, don't you remember? You even apologised to me.'

Pancho hung his head and sheepishly scuffed the ground with

one hoof. At length he turned his head and gazed at Gustave with big, faithful eyes.

'Will you forgive me?' he said in a low voice.

No response. Pancho whinnied in embarrassment.

'All right,' Gustave said eventually. 'I forgive you. But now, tell me how you escaped.'

'No idea,' Pancho blurted out. 'It was like some terrible nightmare. I sank in deeper and deeper, and the ground closed over me. I'm going to suffocate, I thought, but I found I could breathe in spite of all the mud and stones around me. Then, quite suddenly, I felt as if I'd been fired from a cannon. Whoosh! I shot up through the darkness, right through the ground, like a shaft of lightning up a drainpipe. Higher and higher I went, and all at once the darkness lifted: my head emerged from the ground, followed by my neck and the whole of my body. Before I knew it, I was back on terra firma. The next thing that happened was, I noticed *you* sitting astride me once more.'

'Strange things happen in the forest,' mused Gustave.

'We aren't in the forest any longer,' Pancho replied darkly. 'This is the Valley of the Monsters, the land of eternal twilight. I've heard of the place. It's never really daytime here. Twilight falls, then night, then twilight again, then night. Day refuses to illuminate this part of the world, so they say. The sun passes by, but only to set.'

Peering closely at the valley, Gustave made out a number of weird shapes. They seemed to be moving, but at this distance and in the fading light he couldn't tell what they were.

'Those are monsters,' the horse whispered unasked. 'The most monstrous monsters in existence.'

'The most monstrous are just the kind I'm looking for,' said Gustave, and he spurred Pancho down the hill and into the gloomy valley.

The descent took quite a while because Pancho had to proceed slowly, selecting his footholds with care for fear of stumbling. Meanwhile, the moon had risen and was peeping through the clouds from time to time. Grey shapes of unnatural conformation, some with glowing eyes, would suddenly emerge from the darkness when its silvery light fell on them. They squeaked or grunted and were mercifully swallowed up once more by the gloom. Gustave occasionally mistook something for a boulder or a fallen tree, only to see it stirring silently. Long, thin creatures equipped with far too many legs pattered across his route and vanished into the nocturnal shadows.

Gustave more than once heard the rustle of leathery wings circling not far above his head. The darkness was alive with whispers and crackles, high-pitched whistles and distant howls.

'If we're out of luck,' murmured Pancho, his voice filled with apprehension, 'we may run into the Most Monstrous of All Monsters without realising it. It could be looming over us at this very moment, massive as a mountain, with tentacles instead of arms and one huge eye capable of seeing in the dark. You see those tall trees on either side of us? They may not be trees at all—they may be *legs*!'

'Do you mind keeping your flights of fancy to yourself?' Gustave protested. 'If there *are* any monsters lurking in the darkness, I'd like to be able to hear them coming before they attack us.'

At that moment the clouds parted, and they saw that they had for some time been trotting through a vast expanse of ruins. Massive blocks of stone were all that remained of tall buildings that had collapsed long ago, leaving only vestiges of their walls standing.

The route was barred by fallen stones, and Pancho had to pick his way among them with care.

Seen by the moon's pale light, the ruins looked like ice floes wedged together. Perched on top of them were flocks of owls whose big, round eyes reflected the cold light streaming down from the cosmos.

'The result of an earthquake, probably,' said Gustave.

'Monsters is my bet,' was Pancho's awestruck response.

'*Are you wondering what horrific creature wrecked this place?*' The voice that rang out over the dismal landscape was deep, dark and mournful. It sounded as if it were issuing from a dungeon.

Universal panic ensued. Gustave wrenched at the reins and fumbled with his lance, Pancho reared up on his hind legs and wheeled on the spot as though encircled by rats. At that moment a pallid moonbeam pierced the overcast and shone straight down on a monster leaning against a ruined wall only a few yards away. 'It was me,' it said.

The monster had a head like a dragon's skull. Its arms, which were composed of gnarled wood, ended in flexible, plantlike tentacles. The rest of it was mercifully obscured by the wall it was leaning against. More tentacles wriggling through cracks between the stones seemed to suggest that the ruined masonry concealed still more horrific portions of its anatomy.

'Well,' the monster boomed, 'are you paying the Valley of the Monsters a visit?'

A big wolf spider crawled out of its right eye socket and went scuttling down the wall.

'Er, yes,' Gustave answered quickly. 'And a very good evening to you.'

'You're only passing through, I trust, not planning to spend a vacation here. Aren't they awful, these desolate surroundings? These dismal forms of plant life that proliferate everywhere? These depressing climatic conditions? Living here is like stagnating under a steamed-up cheese cover.' The bony skull heaved a deep sigh.

Gustave dismounted. The monster seemed civilised despite its frightful appearance, so he signalled his peaceful intentions by replacing his lance in its sheath and leaving his helmet behind with Pancho. So as to be prepared for certain eventualities, however, he kept his iron skullcap on and retained his swordbelt. With one sweaty hand gripping the hilt of his sword, he clambered over the tilted, uneven blocks of stone that lay between him and the monster.

The monster's chalk-white head peered over the wall like some puppet from a Punch-and-Judy show designed for audiences with exceptionally strong nerves. Gustave strode up to it, took his courage in both hands, and struck a knightly pose.

'Are you the Most Monstrous of All Monsters?' he asked firmly.

Some crunching, sucking noises emanated from the shadows at the foot of the wall. A few tentacles withdrew and reappeared through cracks elsewhere. The huge death's-head rose and fell in an unnatural way, like a carnival mask bobbing on the end of a stick. 'The Most Monstrous of All Monsters?' repeated the monster. 'Yes, I suppose I am . . . ' It paused for effect before continuing: 'Or used to be, long, long ago . . . '

It paused again, seemingly afraid to utter the next words. 'But then another monster came along. Well, it had always been there in reality, but the longer it existed the more monstrous it became. No, the most I am is the Second Most Monstrous of All Monsters. My name is Anxiety.' The monster bowed its head and followed up its statement with another deep sigh like the wheezing of a decrepit pair of bellows.

'Never fear,' it went on without waiting for a response, 'I won't accuse you of being tactless for asking such a direct question. Milk can turn sour at the very sight of me, I know. I nearly fainted once, when I caught sight of my reflection in a pool of water—and I was considerably more attractive then than I am now.'

The monster groaned at the recollection. 'You're bound to be wondering what's so awful about anxiety, right?'

'Er, yes,' said Gustave. Although it wasn't true (he was far too agitated to wonder about anything), he thought it wisest to agree with the monster on principle.

'People take me for granted—that's one of my most disastrous characteristics.' The monster gave a hollow laugh. Stone grated on stone as if the creature were bracing itself against the wall with all its might.

'Look around you and see how effective I've been. I've ravaged this place for many years—ravaged it good and proper. I devour men, women and children regardless of their social class and personal character. I'm ruthless and relentless, cold-blooded and implacable. In short, I'm a servant of Death—one of the best, what's more.'

Gustave pricked up his ears. 'You're a servant of Death?'

'Aren't we all?' Brushing aside his question with a tentacular gesture expressive of boredom, the monster continued its self-revelation. 'In the end, I grew a little weary one day and decided to lean against this wall—only for a moment.'

The skull gave a deep, dry cough.

'Well, as you can see, I'm still here many, many years later, so something *crucial* must have happened to me in the meantime, mustn't it?'

Gustave nodded, but this time not just for courtesy's sake. He was genuinely interested to see what the monster was leading up to.

'I'd begun to *worry*! I'd begun to question the meaning of my existence! Can you imagine? The fact is, *Anxiety was beginning to worry!* Not a particularly clever career move, my boy, I see that now, because it was then that I lost my pre-eminent status as the Most Monstrous of All Monsters.'

'But isn't a touch of self-doubt a good thing at times?' Gustave asked, just to keep the conversational ball rolling.

'Doubt?' exclaimed the monster. 'I'm not talking about a healthy dose of scepticism, my young friend! No, I didn't *doubt*, I *worried*, and they're as different as ... as thinking and dreaming. I started to worry about everything, absolutely everything! I worry about my health, about the future, about the present—even about the past, which is a particularly futile occupation.'

The death's-head emitted a rattling laugh. 'Yes, I started worrying, and that has made me what you see today: dead, dried-up timber, bone, horn, stone, teeth without nerves, eye sockets devoid of eyes.' The monster threw up its wooden tentacles in despair. They trembled pitifully, outlined against the night sky, then collapsed and dangled there inert. The spider came crawling back up the wall and disappeared into the eye socket. The bony skull's lament culminated in a long, inarticulate sigh.

'*This really can't be the Most Monstrous of All Monsters,*' Gustave told himself, '*it's far too much of a cry-baby. I'm only wasting time here.*'

'You're only wasting time here, my boy,' the monster said softly. 'I'm sure I'm boring you with my tales of woe.'

Gustave gave a start. He had a nasty feeling that the monster had looked straight into his head.

'But perhaps I can give you something to take on your way,' the creature went on. 'It's nothing much, philosophically speaking, just a piece of sound advice: Make the most of every moment!'

Gustave had read similar well-meant proverbs on calendars.

'Yes, I know, you've read similar well-meant proverbs on calendars, haven't you? Still, it can't be repeated too often.'

'I'll make a note of it,' Gustave said politely, slowly beginning to back away.

'No, I'm not the Most Monstrous of All Monsters, not any more.' The monster might have been talking to itself. 'I'm still pretty monstrous, but only moderately so by local standards. I'm neither as pathetically unmonstrous as those absurd twin-headed giant snails on the hillsides above this valley, nor as humongously monstrous as the *Knight-Eating Giant Saurian of Lake Blue-Blood*. Me, I'm only averagely monstrous.'

Gustave was suddenly galvanised. He came to a halt.

'The Knight-Eating Giant Saurian of Lake Blue-Blood?' he said. 'That sounds interesting. Sounds as if it could really be the Most Monstrous of All Monsters.'

'Well, that's what it claims to be.'

'Really? Can you tell me where to find the creature?'

'It's quite simple. At the end of the valley, you must ride up into the hills and under the *Weeping Waterfalls* to *Groaning Glen*. From there you make your way across the *Plain of the Terrible Titans* to the *Malodorous Mountains*. Lake Blue-Blood is situated at their most malodorous point.' The monster drew a deep, whistling breath.

'Many thanks,' said Gustave.

'You're welcome.' The monster dismissed this expression of gratitude by waving one of its tentacles. 'But before you go: Didn't you wonder, while listening to my story, whether there was some kind of point to it?'

Gustave gave a tight-lipped smile. 'Oh, I enjoyed it anyway, point or no point.'

'That's good, because there wasn't one.'

Gustave stumbled backwards for a few steps, grinning and waving goodbye. Then he turned, hurried across the ruins to his horse, and climbed into the saddle. Pancho trotted off. As for the monster, it relapsed into its former immobility and became a lonely monument to melancholy once more.

They rode on through the Valley of the Monsters for a long way yet. Their route took them past more dismal ruins and withered vegetation, over countless skeletons, both animal and human, and through the scuttling, squeaking swarms of rats and insects that seemed to have made the rubble-strewn plain their own. But they encountered no more monstrosities apart from two twin-headed giant snails grazing peacefully in the mist at the end of the valley next morning. Between them lay a steeply ascending track that led out of the valley and into the mountains.

Once across the first mountain pass, they were confronted by an awe-inspiring sight: a dark ravine, narrower than the first but considerably deeper. It was enclosed by jagged crags above and filled with billowing clouds of vapour below. Dozens of waterfalls cascaded down the sheer walls of rock, thundering like a never-ending storm and pattering like perpetual rain. Blue-black birds circled above the swirling spray, croaking eerily.

'These must be the Weeping Waterfalls,' said Gustave. 'Not a very pleasant spot, but we've got to get past it somehow.'

'Not very pleasant is putting it mildly,' remarked Pancho, who hadn't failed to notice that their route led *beneath* the waterfalls. Little more than an arm's-breadth wide, it was an uneven ledge interspersed with puddles and slippery with lichen. 'I hope this proves worth the effort,' he added sulkily.

'It had better,' said Gustave. 'My life is at stake.'

'So is mine,' the horse retorted as it teetered along, cautiously testing each foothold in turn.

Their route led upwards, then downwards. On and on they went along the slippery ledge, a sheer drop on their right and the wall of rock on their left. From time to time they had no choice but to plough straight through a waterfall, and Gustave's armour soon filled with gurgling, ice-cold water. Then came a long uphill stretch that made Pancho curse incessantly. At last the rocks suddenly parted to disclose a view of some lush mountain meadows. The grassland sloped down, undulating gently, to a valley through which, to judge by the faint murmur that filled the air, a stream was flowing.

'That must be Groaning Glen!' Gustave exclaimed.

Pancho looked relieved. 'It doesn't seem such a depressing place. I can't hear any groans.'

He stumbled on and, sure enough, they came to a crystal-clear stream flowing through a birchwood gilded with sunlight. Twittering songbirds circled overhead, butterflies and dragonflies fluttered and whirred through the air. Pancho trotted over to the stream to quench his thirst, Gustave dismounted and did likewise. When he swung himself into the saddle once more, he noticed a many-turreted castle perched on a hill overlooking the valley.

'We seem to be back in civilised parts,' he said, wondering how he was going to find the lake-dwelling Most Monstrous of All Monsters in such peaceful surroundings. The countryside seemed to be completely monster-free. 'Perhaps we should pay a visit to that castle up there. Perhaps it's the home of a wise king or a beautiful princess or some other person who can tell us the way to Lake Blue-Blood.'

'Oh, naturally,' sighed Pancho as he trotted off again, making for the castle. 'Of course it's the home of a wise king or a beautiful princess—both, probably, and they're baking you a cake at this very moment.'

But the higher they climbed the further the castle seemed to recede. Repeatedly obscured by dense swathes of mist, it vanished and reappeared in turn, but they never got close enough to make out more than an alluring silhouette. Then the cotton-wool mist swallowed it up altogether. When the mist finally dispersed, Gustave saw that what he had mistaken for a castle was just a bizarre chain of towering crags that bore only a vague resemblance to turrets and battlements.

'Hm, I hesitate to tell you this,' Pancho observed, 'but we've been fooled by a *fata montana*—a mountain mirage.' They had halted on a rocky plateau, bare except for a few clumps of grass.

Gustave groaned.

'It's quite a common phenomenon at high altitudes,' Pancho explained. 'The mountains' resemblance to architectural features, which is often quite pronounced, coupled with poor visibility, the effect of thin air on one's optical nerves, and the suggestibility of the brain, frequently give rise to hallucinations which—'

'Oh, shut up!' snapped Gustave, and silenced the horse by digging his spurs into its flanks. Pancho's pseudoscientific remarks were beginning to get on his nerves.

For some time now, they had been riding across a highland plateau strewn with isolated boulders. They had lost all sense of direction, and Gustave was afraid they were going in a circle. Thin shreds of mist floated among the rocks, grey banks of cloud drifted overhead. Raven-hued birds of frightening dimensions circled above the plain in search of prey. The light was fading fast, and not the smallest sign of civilisation could be discerned anywhere. Gustave and Pancho were dispirited by hunger and fatigue.

'This is a stone desert,' the horse remarked. 'You won't find any cakes here.'

'To tell the truth,' sighed Gustave, 'I'd counted on spending the evening over a good dinner in the semi-civilised company of some lords and ladies. Roast goose and all the trimmings—something of that kind. Maybe a little background music for strings as well.'

'I don't go in for meat-eating, nor for decadent aristocrats, nor for the noises produced by horsehair scraping catgut,' Pancho retorted. 'Mind you, a nosebag of oats wouldn't come amiss.'

They rode doggedly on, and Gustave noticed after they had gone a little way that the rocks were emitting a strange light. They glittered like certain crystals or metals, and the entire plain looked as if it had been dusted with silver. Before Gustave could broach the subject to Pancho, however, a rumbling sound filled the air. The huge boulders started to move and the hard ground trembled underfoot as it might have done in a moderate earthquake. Rolling around and piling up in defiance of every law of nature, the rocks formed themselves into sculptures resembling gigantic snowmen. Then they seemed to soften, liquefy like lava, and take on human form.

Faces appeared in the liquid rock; hands, legs and arms took shape; eyes protruded and teeth were bared; shaggy hair sprouted, thick and stiff as wire. Within moments, six huge figures were standing there. Uncouth, muscular giants, each of whom must have been three times the height of a man, they had wild, unkempt beards and were carrying axes and clubs in their mighty fists.

Gustave and Pancho froze. Of course! the barren plateau they were crossing could only be the Plain of the Terrible Titans!

'I am Giant **Emashtimact**!' boomed one of them, barring Pancho's path.

'I am Giant **Ogliboy**!' called another.

'I am Giant **Hyposhilop**!'

'I am Giant **Somytrona**!'

'I am Giant **Scisyhp**!'

'And I am Giant **Elyogog**!'

The giants had surrounded Gustave and Pancho while introducing themselves.

It suddenly occurred to Gustave that he had to guess their names. 'I'd completely forgotten,' he thought. 'Of course, it's Task Number Three!'

The giants drew nearer, brandishing their weapons.

'What do you want with us?' Gustave asked, all innocent, while feverishly wondering how to get the better of these unmistakably stronger opponents.

'You must guess our names!' the giants called in unison.

'That's easy,' Gustave replied. 'Emashtimact, Ogliboy, Hyposhilop, Somytrona, Scisyhp, and Elyogog. You introduced yourselves just now.'

'Damnation!' swore Elyogog.

'Hell!' grumbled Emashtimact.

The six giants stood there for a moment, looking foolish and exchanging helpless glances. Then they put their heads together, muttering. At length they all shouted 'Of course!' and turned back to Gustave. Ogliboy elbowed his way to the fore.

'Those, er, weren't our real names,' he announced. 'They were, er, anagrams.'

'Quite so, they were only anagrams,' Emashtimact chimed in. 'Not our *real* names.'

'Our *real* names are quite different.'

All the giants nodded eagerly.

'Anagrams?' asked Gustave. He'd heard the word before, but he couldn't immediately place it.

'Anagrams are words in which the original letters have been rearranged,' Pancho whispered. 'These giants are intellectuals, I'm afraid.'

'We certainly are,' Ogliboy confirmed. 'We're scientists, in fact.'

Emashtimact kicked him hard on the shin.

'You idiot!' he hissed.

'Aha!' Pancho whispered. 'Scientists! That was an unintentional tip. They aren't just intellectuals, they're *brainless* intellectuals.'

Gustave thought it over: *Rearranged letters . . . Scientists . . . Emashtimact, Ogliboy, Hyposhilop, Somytrona, Scisyhp, Elyogog. Hm . . .*

'May I ask questions?' he enquired politely.

'Yes, that's part of the game,' Hyposhilop replied.

'Do you have to answer them truthfully?'

'Yes, worse luck. But only with yes or no.'

'Good,' said Gustave. 'First question: do you use instruments in your scientific work?'

'Yes!' Somytrona blurted out. 'I, for example, use a huge telescope! I've been observing you through it for ages. We can see everything from our castle in the clouds,' he added proudly, and levelled his huge forefinger at the fairy-tale building Gustave had spotted from the bottom of the valley. It had reappeared, curiously enough, complete with all its turrets and battlements, which were now only thinly wreathed in mist. But Gustave had no time to marvel.

'Nothing escapes me!' Somytrona boomed. 'My telescope magnifies things a hundred billion times. I could even see an ant urinating on Saturn.'

'*Are* there ants on Saturn?'

'Of course,' Somytrona replied, somewhat more affably now. 'There are ants everywhere. Admittedly, the ones on Saturn have three heads and urinate mercury, but . . .'

A telescope. Scientists. Somytrona. Mostronya. Yanostrom. Somynator. Antymoros. Ramostony. Ostyomarn . . .

'You own a telescope and observe the stars. Somytrona, your real name is **Astronomy**!'

'Damnation!' said Astronomy. The other giants shook their fists at him for being such a blabbermouth.

'Now you,' Gustave commanded sternly, pointing to Ogliboy. *Yolibog. Iblygoo. Loygibo . . .*

'You! Do you have a telescope too?'

'No!' Ogliboy said triumphantly. 'I have a *microscope*!'

'Shut up, you fool!' bellowed the other giants. 'You only need say yes or no.'

'So you've got a microscope,' Gustave reasoned. 'Do you also use it to observe ants on Saturn?'

'No! With my microscope I observe ants on the earth!'

'Aha!' said Gustave. *Possesses a microscope. Oiglybo. Boligoy. Ligoboy. Observes ants. Bygiloo. Loibygo. Ibogoyl . . .*

'Ogliboy, your name is **Biology**!'

'Confound it!' Biology exclaimed. He kicked the nearest rock so hard, it shattered into a thousand fragments.

'You're next!' Gustave pointed to the strongest and dirtiest-looking giant.

'Elyogog, you look the strongest—you've got the biggest calluses on your hands and the most dirt under your boots. Are your hands and feet your most important tools?'

'Er, yes, as a matter of fact,' Elyogog was compelled to admit.

'Touché!' Pancho said admiringly.

Oglygoe. Legoyog. Eglogoy . . .

'Do you like grubbing around in the dirt?'

The giant blushed and bowed his head.

'Yes,' he said.

Likes grubbing around in the dirt. Yologeg. Oyglego. Golygoe . . .

'And the dirt on your boots—you like walking. Do you get around a lot?'

'Yes,' muttered the giant.

Yogoleg. Gets around a lot. Goylego. Yelgogo. Olygoge . . .

'Your name is **Geology**!'

'Correct,' growled Geology. The other giants booed him.

Gustave pointed to the next giant. He was beginning to like this game.

'You, Emashtimact, what tools do you use?'

'You'll have to guess that yourself. I'm only answering yes or no.'

'That's right!' cried the other giants. 'You tell him!'

'Aha,' said Gustave. 'You work in a logical way. Yours is a very exact science, am I right?'

'Yes, correct.'

'Good. Do you use a metronome?'

Emashtimact laughed. 'Never!'

Metasmicath . . .

'A sextant?'

'Not that either.'

Mamethastic . . .

'A Bunsen burner?'

'Wrong again.'

Masthmacite . . .

'How much is six hundred and twenty-four thousand five hundred and twenty-eight divided by two hundred and thirty-six?'

'I'm not saying,' Emashtimact retorted defiantly. 'I only answer questions you can answer with a yes or a no.'

'Hm,' said Gustave. 'Then answer me this: *Could* you tell me what six hundred and twenty-four thousand five hundred and twenty-eight divided by two hundred and thirty-six makes?'

'Yes, of course,' said Emashtimact.

'Oh, no you couldn't!'

'Oh, yes I could!'

'I don't believe you,' said Gustave. 'No one could do a sum like that in their head.'

'I don't have to!' cried the giant. 'I've got my slide rule for that!' Without thinking, he produced a wooden slide rule from his pocket and triumphantly brandished it aloft.

Stahimemtac. Ishmatectam. Tactamemish . . .

'So you use a slide rule . . . Then your name is **Mathematics**.'

The giant hurled his instrument at the ground and stamped on it.

Gustave turned to the penultimate candidate.

'Now for you, Hyposhilop.'

'Take care, he'll try to hoodwink you!' chorused the other five giants.

'Do you also use an instrument in your branch of learning?' Gustave asked sharply.

'No,' Hyposhilop replied with a grin. 'Mine doesn't need any.'

'Well said!' cried the other giants. 'That's the spirit!'

A science that needs no instruments. Olyphoship. Hopyliposh. Polyshipho . . .

'Why doesn't it need any instruments?'

'Because it deals with something no instrument can measure— whoops!'

Hyposhilop clapped a hand over his mouth as if the answer had already slipped out.

'Careful, you fool!' yelled the other giants.

A science dealing with something no instruments can measure. Hospophily. Shylopoiph. Phyloshoip. Sholopiphy . . .

'Then your name is **Philosophy**,' Gustave decided, 'and you're no smarter than the others.'

'Hey, this is fun,' Pancho whinnied. 'Can I guess the last one?'

'No!' Gustave said sternly. 'That's my job.'

'Hey, what about me?' called Scisyhp. 'You won't catch *me* out with your trick questions! You'll never guess *my* name!'

'Oh, Scisyhp,' Gustave said with a pitying smile. 'I'd entirely forgotten about you. You're far too easy, that's why. I've no need to ask you any questions. Only seven letters, and you haven't even taken the trouble to jumble them up properly, just turned them back to front. Your name is **Physics**, of course.'

'We told you so!' growled the other giants. 'You nitwit!'

Gustave was in the best of spirits. He had taken on six huge giants—scientists and intellectuals into the bargain—and defeated them in a battle of wits. Another of Death's tasks had been completed. He tugged at the reins—Pancho reared up on his hind legs—and raised a hand in farewell.

'Well, gentlemen, that's it. I've guessed your names, so I'll take my leave. Have a nice evening.'

He was about to steer Pancho between Mathematics and Biology when they closed up and barred his route.

'One moment,' said Mathematics.

'What is it?' Gustave said impatiently. 'I've got other tasks to perform.'

'Not so fast, my lad.' There was a menacing undertone in Biology's amiable voice. 'Haven't you forgotten something?'

'Forgotten something?' hissed Pancho. 'Like what?'

'What do you mean?' Gustave demanded.

Astronomy cleared his throat.

'We've been observing you all the time through my huge telescope, as I told you. To our dismay, we've discovered that you haven't done your homework—in biology and astronomy, mathematics and physics, philosophy and geology. *That's* what you've forgotten!'

The other giants grunted approvingly.

It was true: Gustave had recently got a little behindhand with his homework. He was normally a hard-working and ambitious pupil, however, so he felt no need to reproach himself on that score.

'Well?' he said.

'Instead of doing your homework, you sit there and *scribble*,' Mathematics said in accusing tones.

'I don't scribble,' Gustave retorted defiantly, 'I *draw*!'

'Draw?' exclaimed Biology. 'You won't get anywhere in life like that. Drum the rudiments of the monopodial ramifications of umbelliferous plants into your head, and you could go far.'

'Precisely!' said Mathematics. 'The same goes for the binomial theorem. It's an absolute must in everyday life, yet you waste your precious time on anatomical studies.'

'I'm genuinely concerned,' said Physics. 'How can you possibly hope to lead a well-ordered life without knowing how to conduct an effective spectral analysis?'

'I aim to earn my living as an artist,' Gustave replied stoutly.

The giants pulled commiserating faces and nudged each other in the ribs.

'The poor, deluded youth!' Physics exclaimed.

Geology shook his head. 'Just fancy, he proposes to go through life without knowing the difference between the Pleistocene, the Cretaceous and the Jurassic!'

'He'd sooner *draw*!' The giants roared with laughter until the ground shook. Gustave debated whether to spur Pancho into a gallop and make a dash for it, but he knew the giants would overhaul him within a few strides. Having recovered their breath, they looked down at him gravely and wagged their heads.

'We simply want to spare you a life of hardship and disgrace, my boy,' Geology said sympathetically. 'That's why we're going to trample you to death with our granite boots.'

The giants drew nearer, Pancho whinnied and retreated. Gustave gripped the reins more tightly and compelled him to stand still.

'Why should you trample me to death?' he demanded.

'Because it's the custom on the Plain of the Terrible Titans,' Biology replied. 'You come our way, we make you pay.'

'*He comes our way, we make him pay!*' chanted the other giants.

'You come up here, it costs you dear!' cried Geology.

'*He comes up here, it costs him dear!*'

The giants began to stamp their feet rhythmically, revealing the dirt-encrusted soles of their boots. They broke into another chant:

Do you hear our fearsome chorus?
You are just the victim for us!
We shall trample you to death,
squeeze out every ounce of breath!

They pranced round Gustave and Pancho in a circle, clapping their hands, and the plain shuddered in time to the stomping of their granite boots. Philosophy paused for a moment and bent over Gustave.

'Do you see the way the plain shimmers?' he asked.

Gustave had, of course, already been struck by the silvery film that coated the stony ground.

'That's the remains of all the suits of armour we've trampled to dust, together with their occupants. It's the silver dust from all those dead knights which makes the plain shimmer like that.' Philosophy laughed and took up the refrain once more.

Like quicksilver gleam you must
when we've trampled you to dust.
Come, young man, it's growing late,
so prepare to meet your fate.

The giants sang and stamped in a mounting frenzy as they steadily converged on Gustave.

'*Late, late!*' chorused the gargantuan creatures.

'*Fate, fate!*' came the echo from the mountains around.

'It's time you used one of your confounded weapons,' Pancho hissed. 'Lance, sword, armour—why else have I been toting them around all this time? You're a knight, damn it all, so kindly act like one!'

Gustave drew his sword.

The giants were unimpressed. '*Fate, fate!*' they bellowed.

'What now?' asked Gustave.

'Just do as I say,' Pancho whispered. 'Hold your sword out in front of you, parallel to the ground, and keep it there. Grip it as tightly as you can.'

The giants joined hands like children playing ring o' roses. '*Must, must, dust, dust!*' they chanted.

'And now?' Gustave whispered. 'Shall I run them through?'

'No, no,' Pancho muttered between his teeth. 'Just let them come closer.'

'Even closer? They'll crush us to death any minute.' Gustave was still reluctant to take orders from a horse.

'Don't lose your nerve,' Pancho whispered. 'Let them come closer. Hold your arm out straight and keep absolutely still.'

'*Die, die!*' yelled the steadily advancing giants, feet pounding. '*You must die!*'

All at once, Pancho rose on his hind legs. 'Ever heard of an admirable Japanese custom known as *seppuku*?' he called loudly. Then he whirled on the spot—so swiftly, gracefully and unexpectedly that Gustave himself was taken by surprise.

His adversaries were considerably more surprised, because all six discovered that they had been cut in half. Pancho's pirouette had sent Gustave's sword slicing through their bellies, neatly severing the upper halves of their bodies from the lower. The bisected giants lay on the ground, screaming and groaning, while their lower halves ran around aimlessly, like headless chickens. Their innards overflowed their waists and oozed along the ground, the blood came welling out of their stomachs in thick red rivulets.

'Not a very appetising sight,' said Pancho, on the verge of throwing up. 'Let's get out of here before I vomit.'

Gustave sheathed his sword, applied the spurs, and Pancho galloped off across the plain at full tilt. Before long, when they were far enough away to be spared the sound of the giants' groans and curses, Pancho slowed to a leisurely trot.

'That was child's play,' said Gustave.

'Yes, giants are easy meat provided you get them in the right place. Their midriffs are quite soft. Mind you, the sword has to be forged by a master craftsman and sharp as a razor.'

'How could you have known the blade was so sharp?'

'Because your weapons were personally supplied by Death, and there's one thing you can depend on: if Death supplies you with something, he quality-controls it himself. He must still be hoping

you'll despair of completing your tasks and fall on your sword, or something.'

Gustave heaved a sigh. 'It's nice to have friends.'

'Hey,' said Pancho, 'we forgot to ask those giants the way to Lake Blue-Blood.'

At last they began to descend a rocky slope flanked by towering granite peaks that resembled the petrified horns of a herd of cyclopean bulls. Far below, wreathed in mist, lay a lake.

'Could that be Lake Blue-Blood?' Gustave wondered aloud.

'I don't detect any unpleasant smell,' Pancho said breathlessly, 'so we can't have reached the Malodorous Mountains yet.'

'The lake is blue,' Gustave pointed out.

'Mountain lakes generally are,' Pancho replied. 'That doesn't mean it's Lake Blue-Blood, far from it.'

'Do you think Lake Blue-Blood is really full of blood?'

'Nothing would surprise me in these accursed mountains.'

They rode past a steep rocky outcrop surmounted by a ruined watchtower with crows fluttering round it.

'At least we're nearing civilisation again,' Gustave said. 'Hey, can you smell it too?'

Pancho came to a halt and sniffed the air.

'That's not a smell,' he snorted, 'it's an *outrage*.'

'Sulphur,' Gustave decided. 'Where the air smells of sulphur, volcanic activity is to be expected. Let's ride over to that promontory—we should get a good view of the lake from there.'

Pancho obediently trotted off. When they looked over the edge of the cliff, their view of the lake was even more appalling than its stench. No doubt about it: they had reached the Malodorous Mountains at last. In many places, gas bubbles rising to the viscous surface burst with a loud pop. Foaming in the middle of the lake was a volcanic whirlpool, and the water near its shores was boiling hot. The acrid fumes and concentrated odour of sulphur it gave off were so strong, they made both horse and rider heave. What mainly caused Pancho to recoil several steps, however, was the sight of all the monsters.

The waters and shores of the lake—even the rugged cliffs that enclosed it—were teeming with them. Wyverns undulated through the water, giant hippopotamuses floated in it like islands; the mountain lake and its immediate vicinity were populated by every conceivable form of nightmarish beast, from many-headed serpents and primeval raptors to octopuses of monstrous size.

Wherever one looked, hair-raisingly hideous creatures wriggled and wallowed, fluttered and crawled. Equipped with scales and horns, suckers and talons, wings and fangs, spiked tails and yards-long tongues, they scrambled up the cliffs to inspect Gustave and his steed as soon as they caught sight of them. A spider the size of Pancho came scuttling up the sheer rock face at an alarming rate and planted itself in front of them, brandishing its forelegs in an aggressive manner and hissing through its venom-laden mandibles. Low-flying creatures of the air circled Gustave on leathery wings, and more and more monstrosities came to the surface of the lake to greet the newcomers.

But the most frightful monster of all could be seen in the middle of the lake. A crocodile of prehistoric proportions, it could only be the Knight-Eating Giant Saurian. Why? Because it was in the act of devouring a knight, complete with horse and armour, while the hapless man's squire—or what was left of him—was being chewed up by the beak of a huge, vulture-like bird perched on a rock below Gustave and Pancho.

'I reckon we're in the right place,' Gustave whispered.

Pancho looked indignant. 'Nothing was ever said about horses being eaten too!'

'Let's get down to business right away,' Gustave said resolutely. 'Hey!' he shouted across the lake. 'Hey, giant crocodile! Are you the Most Monstrous of All Monsters?'

'Monsters, monsters, monsters!' the Echo Demons shouted back from their rocky niches on the opposite shore.

The crocodile bolted the knight and his horse in two big gulps and belched disgustingly. Then it focused its yellowish-green gaze on Gustave. 'Do you *have* to shout like that?' the giant saurian protested, casting its eyes up to heaven. 'The acoustics here are excellent, my friend. There's no reason why we shouldn't converse in a civilised manner.' Its voice had sunk almost to a whisper. 'But to answer your question: Yes, I *am* the Most Monstrous of All Monsters.'

Gustave indicated the lake with his lance.

'What makes you so much more monstrous than all the other frightful monsters here?' he asked in a quieter voice. 'They're pretty monstrous too.'

'Good question,' Pancho said approvingly.

'Well,' the crocodile replied with a grin, baring a long row of razor-sharp molars, 'there's a small but important difference between them and me. Their motives for murdering and devouring their prey are base and contemptible. They kill out of greed, hunger, or boredom. Or simply out of blood-lust.'

The crocodile seemed to speak without having to open its huge jaws; its cheek muscles twitched a little, but that was all. Its hoarse, gurgling voice, which came from somewhere deep in its intestines, sounded as if it were issuing from a waterlogged grave.

'I, on the other hand, don't kill and eat people from necessity. It isn't pleasure or greed that prompts me to devour them, either. I don't do it out of spite, *I do it for love.*' A soft, dreamy note had come into the crocodile's voice.

'For love?' asked Gustave, clutching his heart.

'Yes, it's the worst thing one can do,' sighed the crocodile. 'It breaks my heart every time. A shooting pain transfixes my breast like a dagger-thrust, and—'

'I know the sensation well,' Gustave said sadly.

'Then you understand me!' breathed the crocodile. 'You know how I feel! I always weep when I devour my prey. You see this lake? It isn't water, it's crocodile tears, each of them personally shed by me. The blue coloration comes from the knights' noble blood.'

'How can you love someone you devour?' Gustave demanded suspiciously. 'How can you devour someone you love?'

'You want to know how love works?' The saurian groaned. 'You'd better ask someone else, then. *I* certainly don't know. Why do I kill what I love? Yes, why *do* I? *You* tell *me!*' From inside the crocodile came a mournful gurgle like the intake of breath between two sobs. 'But the really inexplicable thing,' it went on, 'is not that *I* love those whom I devour. The inexplicable, utterly amazing thing is that the people I devour love *me* although they know I'm going to devour them. Indeed, they actually love me *while* I'm devouring them!'

'Nonsense,' snorted Pancho.

'I don't believe it,' Gustave said firmly.

'Then come a step closer,' cooed the crocodile. 'Come on, I can demonstrate it to you.'

'It only wants to grab us with its long snout,' Pancho growled between his teeth. 'Crocodiles can jump, so I've heard.'

'We're far too high up,' Gustave decreed. 'We can risk going one step closer.' He jabbed his lance at the giant spider, which uttered a venomous hiss but cravenly retreated and took refuge in a crack lower down the cliff. Pancho took a hesitant step towards the edge.

'You see?' said the crocodile. 'I won't harm you. This isn't a trap—I won't try any dirty tricks. You can trust me.' Its voice had acquired an entirely new quality. Although clearer, more penetrating and easier to understand, it sounded softer and gentler than before—like a whisper breathed straight into Gustave's ear.

'Hm,' said Gustave. 'This crocodile is an honest creature. It hasn't even tried to jump up at us.'

'It certainly seems to be on the level,' Pancho conceded. 'In my view, it makes a thoroughly likeable impression.'

'We could be the best of friends,' cooed the crocodile, and its voice reverberated soothingly inside Gustave's head like the purring of a cat. 'We could do all kinds of things together.'

Gustave couldn't understand it. His long-standing prejudice against crocodiles now struck him as quite absurd. Crocodiles were genuinely amiable, sensitive creatures. Their armour might be tough, but it clearly concealed a soft heart. The prospect of engaging in some form of joint activity with this nice crocodile filled him with eager anticipation.

'What kind of things could we do, for instance?' he asked.

'Well,' said the monster, 'you could jump into the lake, so I could eat you. I'd toy with you for a while—I'd confine myself at first to biting off your arms and legs, so you could witness the whole procedure. Then I'd chew up your head and scatter your innards across the lake for the others to devour.' The crocodile's voice resembled wavelets breaking on a distant shore—a soft, reassuring sound that filled Gustave's head and gently dispelled any remaining doubts or misgivings. He would happily have conveyed his assent by throwing his arms around the creature's neck. His liking for it, which had increased by leaps and bounds in the past few moments, transcended mere affection. He blushed.

'That's an excellent suggestion,' he said rather sheepishly. 'How about it, Pancho? Shall we jump into the lake?'

'Of course,' said Pancho, who was gazing at the crocodile with rapture, 'but only if I get eaten too. Could that be arranged?'

'I'm pretty full already,' the monster gurgled, 'but I've still got room for half a horse or so. I could at least rip your belly open and nibble your guts a bit.'

'Then what are we waiting for?' Pancho cried eagerly. 'Let's go!'

He pranced backwards another two steps, flexed his hind legs, and got ready to jump. Very slowly and without a sound, the crocodile opened its huge jaws to reveal a glistening green tongue awash with slime and blue blood. Surrounding it were mountain ranges of sharp-edged teeth with shreds of knightly armour lodged between them.

Gustave let go of the reins and dug his spurs in. 'We're coming!' he cried joyously.

Pancho bounded towards the edge of the precipice. The monsters in the lake emitted a collective sigh, a voluptuous sound expressive of avid anticipation. Strangely enough, the sound trans-fixed Gustave's chest like an icy blade. At the same time, a thought shot through his mind: *How can I love the Most Monstrous of All Monsters if my heart belongs to the beautiful damsel?* Something inside him seemed to rip like canvas. Feeling faint, he clutched his chest, lost his balance, and fell off just as Pancho leapt boldly over the cliff. He landed on his back with a clatter of armour, but crawled to the edge on all fours as fast as he could. From below came a pandemonium of splashing, whinnying and grunting. Gustave was just in time to see Pancho disappear, hindquarters first, into the monster's maw. There was a blissful—nay, ecstatic—expression on the horse's face.

'I love this crocodile!' Pancho cried fervently. Then he was gone.

The saurian's jaws closed with a snap. It gave a huge gulp, then redirected its attention to Gustave.

'Well, what are you waiting for?' it cooed, gazing at him lovingly. 'Why don't you jump?'

'I, er,' Gustave said haltingly. 'My heart . . . '

The crocodile's heavy eyelids drooped.

'Oh, no,' it groaned, 'don't tell me your heart belongs to another?' Gustave nodded.

'Well, well, so you're a *genuine knight errant*, eh?' The creature's tone was coldly contemptuous now.

Gustave seemed to awaken from a trance. What had he almost done? What had happened to Pancho? Why was he crawling about on all fours, talking to a crocodile?

'Not bad, eh, that trick with my voice?' the monster said with a grin. 'No idea how I do it, but it works every time. Must be some kind of acoustic hypnosis. I could join a circus.'

Gustave scrambled to his feet. 'It seems you really are the Most

Monstrous of All Monsters,' he called. Thunder rumbled in the distance, and he noticed that the crocodile kept glancing nervously at the sky.

'You've eaten my horse,' he went on, his voice trembling with rage and determination. He drew his sword. 'I'm going to come down and kill you and take one of your teeth. You've asked for it, Most Monstrous of All Monsters!'

'Hush, not so loud!' whispered the crocodile.

'What is it? What are you talking about?'

'That bit about the Most Monstrous of All Monsters. Perhaps you wouldn't mind lowering your voice a little.'

'What do you mean? You *are* **the Most Monstrous of All Monsters**, aren't you?' Gustave had no intention of lowering his voice. It was thundering loudly now.

'Ssh!' hissed the crocodile.

'**Answer me, Most Monstrous of All Monsters!**'

Gustave was in a rage. His injunction was underlined by a violent thunderclap.

'Er, well, *of course* I'm a monstrous monster, but . . . well, I'm only averagely monstrous,' the crocodile mumbled, gritting its teeth and anxiously scanning the sky with its saurian eyes.

'Just a minute!' Gustave exclaimed. 'Does that mean you aren't the Most Monstrous of All Monsters at all?'

The sky above the seething lake was growing dark. Propelled across it by fierce gusts of wind, grey clouds circled over the valley in ever darker, ever denser spirals. All the monsters on the rocky shore dived headlong into the lake. The giant spider toppled backwards out of its crack, fell through the air, and sank beneath the seething surface, frantically waving its legs. The crocodile gave a furious snarl, and remnants of its penultimate meal—a head, a foot, a mailed arm—came flying out of its mouth. It lashed its tail wildly, then dived head first into the blue waves, creating a gurgling whirlpool that sucked the few other remaining monsters into the depths. Within a few moments, there was no sign that the lake had once been alive with them.

Out of the whirling clouds there now came a menacing sound, a loud grunting and panting that drowned the roar of the wind and the rumble of the thunder.

The clouds parted like a curtain, and through the dark cleft between them came a creature that almost defied description. It was too grotesque to seem genuinely malign and too hideous to be comical. Bigger than any dragon, it was a pig with the clawed forefeet of a lizard, the hind legs of a goat, a serpent's tail, and the wings of an eagle.

With a few majestic wing-beats, it swooped down and hovered above the cliff on which Gustave was standing.

A dark swirl of cloud, which had followed the creature down, dispersed beneath it into a pall of mist swarming with vague grey forms. They seemed to materialise from one moment to the next, only to disappear once more, forever merging or passing through one another.

'*I* **am the Most Monstrous of All Monsters**,' snorted the flying pig—less to Gustave, it seemed, than to the monsters lurking in Lake Blue-Blood, for its voice was excessively loud. '**I, and I alone!**'

Gustave had to summon up all his courage to accost the creature, but it was high time to clarify the situation.

'With respect,' he said, 'several different individuals have already made the same claim, so I really must insist on proof. No offence intended, but I've just seen some even more monstrous-looking creatures—a spider the size of a horse, for instance.'

The huge pig's dark eyes gave Gustave a lingering look. Then it sighed and said, in a perceptibly milder voice, 'Aesthetic criteria aren't the issue here.' There followed a pensive grunt, as if the creature were marshalling its thoughts in preparation for a lengthy dissertation.

'It's a question of *effect*, not appearance,' it went on. 'I possess the wings of an angel and the face of a demon. My skin resembles the coarsest sandpaper and my tongue ... oh, I can't remember what my terrible tongue consists of! I eat everything: meat and vegetable matter, mud and sand, wood and stone, iron and gold, stars and planets. I eat water and air. I devour light itself, and I'll also devour *you*. I'm already doing so, in fact, though you're still too young to notice. One day I shall choke on myself and the universe will implode—not that you'll be there to witness the event. No one will.'

Gustave found this such a thoroughly self-assured and impressive performance, all he could think of to do was to ask, in a subdued voice, 'So who exactly are you?'

'I am **Time**!' the winged monster squealed triumphantly, and the grey shapes beneath it milled around in a state of even greater agitation.

'Those,' the Time Pig explained, indicating the nebulous figures, 'are my army of microseconds.' It made a dismissive gesture with its claw-tipped forefoot. 'They're just moments, instants, twinklings of an eye, cannon fodder. I get through vast numbers of them.'

The pig fluttered down, landed on the cliff in front of Gustave, and remained standing on its hind legs. It was many times his height.

'So much for me, but who are you? Who is it that wants to make the acquaintance of the Most Monstrous of All Monsters?'

'My name is Gustave. Gustave Doré.'

'Never heard of you,' said the Time Pig, enveloping him in a miasma of foul-smelling breath.

'That's not surprising,' said Gustave. 'I'm still pretty young, so I haven't had a chance to make a name for myself. I'm not here of my own free will, either. I was sent by Death.'

'Death?' the Time Pig thundered. '*That* silly ass? What's he after *this* time? He'd do better to carve his soul-coffins and attend to that demented sister of his.'

'So you aren't a servant of Death?'

'No. Yes. No. Er, that's to say ... What a stupid question! I'm no one's servant! Death and I, er ... We cooperate from time to time, but that's all.' The Time Pig looked irritated. 'Anyway, what business is it of *yours*?'

'Well,' Gustave said haltingly, 'it's a long and complicated story. All right, to be frank—please don't be angry!—I'm supposed to extract one of your teeth.' There, the truth was out.

The huge pig's whole demeanour changed in a flash. It bent down and looked at Gustave with an expression of mingled pain and hope.

'You want to pull one of my teeth?' it grunted. 'That would be a godsend!' It opened its jaws, enabling Gustave to see far into its maw. 'The thing is, one of my molars is badly abscessed. The whole of the root has filled up with sulphur. You see the stench that comes out of my mouth? It's almost unendurable.'

Gustave peered into the creature's mouth. It was true: he could not only smell but actually see the effluvium that rose from the right-hand side of the lower jaw. Like fumes from the crater of a volcano, it was issuing from an exceptionally rotten tooth flanked by other neglected brown stumps.

'I've never managed to persuade anyone to relieve me of it,' the Time Pig went on. 'If you'd take on the job, I'd be more than grateful.'

Gustave ventured another look into the stinking mouth. The smell almost knocked him backwards, and he couldn't help retching.

'I'll do it,' he said manfully, '—as long as I can keep the tooth when it's out.'

'Say no more!' the Time Pig exclaimed. 'Of course you can have the confounded thing. I'll be glad to be rid of it.'

'Then please go down on all fours,' said Gustave, drawing his sword. 'And open your mouth a bit wider.'

The Time Pig complied. It hinged down its lower jaw, and Gustave bravely planted one foot on the slimy tongue, which really did look as if no one could have told what it consisted of. The stench was almost unbearable, but Gustave tried to hold his breath and act as quickly as possible. Inserting the tip of his sword between the gum and the neck of the tooth, he called, 'This may hurt a bit!' and resolutely thrust it in. The blade severed several nerves, the pig gave an agonised grunt, the ruined tooth's crater vented a jet of blood and pus the thickness of a man's arm. Gustave was un-deterred. Using the sword as a lever, he threw his full weight against it and prised the rotten tooth from its inflamed socket with a sound like a gumboot being yanked out of a bog. Then he seized hold of the tooth, severed the remaining nerves, and, gasping for breath, regained the open air.

The Time Pig reared up with a groan, then doubled up in pain, whimpering and wailing and flapping its wings hysterically. Meanwhile, Gustave carefully wiped the tooth clean on some tufts of grass and stowed it inside his breastplate.

'Well,' he said, 'feeling better?'

The monster, which had quietened a little, was moaning and clutching its right cheek. 'That was a unique experience,' it groaned. 'Many thanks, though. I do feel considerably better.'

'I'm glad,' said Gustave. He decided to get down to brass tacks. 'Would you think it very impolite of me to ask you a favour in return?'

'You've already got the tooth,' the Time Pig grunted. 'Besides, I'm very busy.'

'It's only another question,' said Gustave. 'My next task is to meet myself, and I've no idea how to set about it.'

'That's impossible,' the Time Pig said meditatively.

'I know.'

'Let me finish! It's only impossible so long as you're in your own spatio-temporal continuum. If you changed your continuum, however, you could see your *spatio-temporal continuum projection* in your *future-contingency honeycomb*, which would more or less amount to meeting yourself.'

'I don't understand. What's a spatio-temporal, er . . .'

'Spatio-temporal continuum projection? It gives you a view of your future-contingency time warp. In other words . . . Well, I really can't explain that either. But I can take you there.'

'Really?'

'Of course. All we have to do is take a trip into the future.'

'Could you do that?'

'Hey,' the pig exclaimed, 'I'm *Time*, remember?'

Gustave seated himself on the Time Pig's back. It spat a little blood and pus into Lake Blue-Blood, then flapped its leathery wings and took off. Above the clouds within moments, they climbed higher and higher. Time gave another flap of its wings, and they left the earth's atmosphere behind. The strange pair were surrounded on all sides by a colossal black void sprinkled with stars that glittered so brightly they hurt Gustave's eyes. Behind them, the earth shrank to a steadily dwindling bluish-white ball.

'I say,' Gustave exclaimed, 'I can breathe! I thought there wasn't any air in space.'

'Nonsense,' the Time Pig replied, 'there's everything in space. They also claim there's no sound here. If that were so, how could you hear me?'

Gustave was surprised at how good the acoustics were in space. He could hear the sun crackling as it burned, and even distant stars rustled like tissue paper. They were just flying past the moon, and he thought he detected a light twinkling at the bottom of one of its craters.

'The Sea of Tranquillity,' the Time Pig said, unasked. 'That's Death's house. The light's on, so he must be at home.'

Before Gustave could reply, the Time Pig flapped its wings several times and they soared past half a dozen planets, some more moons, and a large shower of asteroids. For a while they glided through another black void dimly lit by a few tiny suns in the far distance. Then the specks of light multiplied and condensed until they eventually formed whole constellations in which Gustave seemed to discern familiar shapes, for instance a galloping horse that aroused painful memories of Pancho Sansa. Events had followed one another in such quick succession, he hadn't got around to mourning the loss of his faithful companion.

'Yes, that's the universe for you,' the Time Pig pontificated. 'I mean, we're in it when we're down on earth, but you don't realise that until you're floating around up here, eh? Not even a telescope can convey this sublime impression.'

'You're right,' murmured Gustave, overwhelmed by the boundless panorama.

'But don't be too impressed, my boy. Majestic as it may look from here, the structure of the universe is no more complicated than . . .' Time searched around for a comparison. 'Than that of a department store, for instance.'

Gustave remembered the old woman in the forest, who had also blathered about a department store.

'There are three floors, and a different time prevails on each. The basement contains the past—it's the storeroom, so to speak, where all that has happened is stacked. The ground floor is the present, where we are right now, and the first floor is reserved for the future—everything that's going to happen. Or rather, everything that *may* happen. That's our destination.'

'I once met an old woman who also claimed that the world of dreams was like a department store—if I understood her correctly.'

'I hope she wasn't a dream princess!' The Time Pig laughed. 'The members of that profession like to theorise that the whole of the universe is a dream. A thoroughly subjective interpretation, but quite an interesting philosophy.'

'If that were right,' mused Gustave, '*who* would dream it?'

'Exactly. That would be the next big question: Who is the universe actually dreamt by? Hard to say. By me, perhaps? That would be another very subjective assumption.' The Time Pig gave a grunt of amusement. 'But I'm not dreaming. I don't even sleep. Who knows, perhaps it's a collective dream—perhaps it's a kind of porridge stirred by many dreamers. Not a very appetising idea, what?'

Gustave nodded. A meteor not much bigger than his head wobbled past only an arm's-length away. It was strewn with miniature volcanic craters, one of which was emitting a dainty little flame.

'But perhaps the universe is being dreamt by *you*,' said the Time Pig. 'Who knows?'

Gustave frowned. 'I'm certainly not asleep at the moment,' he said, 'so how can I be dreaming it?'

'Right again. Which brings us back to our original question: Who is the universe dreamt by? At least the two of us can be ruled out as suspects. Perhaps it's dreamt by an ant that lives on Saturn.'

'Are there really ants on Saturn?'

'Of course, there are ants everywhere. Did you know that the ants on Saturn have three heads?'

'Yes,' said Gustave.

'You're a strange lad. You don't know for sure there are ants on Saturn, yet you know they have three heads.'

Gustave could have enlightened the Time Pig, but he refrained. Instead, he asked, 'What if the person who's dreaming it all wakes up?'

The pig gave another laugh. 'In that case, my boy, it's curtains!'

Some more little meteors wobbled past, somewhat faster than the first, and Gustave seemed to hear a noise, a roaring, pattering sound like that of a waterfall. Or was it the crackle of a big fire? A sun?

'We're nearly there!' cried the Time Pig. 'You'd better hold on tight now. We could soon be in for some turbulence.'

A massive asteroid went thundering over their heads. Gustave felt as if he were being tugged at by some mighty, invisible hand that had closed around him and the pig and was towing them along by main force.

'Are we there? Where are we?'

'You see that red dot over there? The one with the orange aura?'

'Yes. Is it a star?'

'No, it's a Galactic Gully. We're taking a short cut, it'll be quicker. Gullies are a bit bumpy, but they're faster than those sluggish black holes. You don't get transformed into light or elasticated like spaghetti, either. You retain your original shape. All that happens is, the words sometimes come out longer when you speak.'

'What is a Galactic Gully?'

'It's the Milky Way's drainpipe, so to speak. An elevator into the future, a slide that'll take you into the day after tomorrow. I told you: up here there's everything. Black holes, white holes, red holes. I once saw a hole near Betelgeuze whose colour I couldn't even find a name for.'

Meanwhile, the red dot had expanded into a purple vortex that occupied half Gustave's field of vision. Spiralling through it, and glowing like molten lava, was a long, dark red streak.

'That looks like Wanderlust Wine,' said Gustave, 'only much bigger.'

'Wanderlust Wine?' The Time Pig chuckled. 'Sounds like a drink I could use a swig of right now.'

'It's very beautiful.'

'Yes, dangerous things often are.'

The roar had swelled to ear-splitting proportions. Gustave saw the vortex capture swarms of meteors, comets, moons and whole planets. They were sucked into its rotating centre and vanished without trace. He felt as if he were being flayed alive.

'Hang on tight!' the Time Pig yelled.

They plunged into the purple whirlpool, and Gustave's head was filled with its crackling, crepitating roar. He saw stars: black, white, yellow, red, orange, green, yellow, blue, lilac, gold, silver, and red again. He went hot and cold and hot in turn. Then everything disintegrated into innumerable multicoloured snowflakes that formed whirling patterns of breathtaking beauty. Simultaneously, absolute silence fell.

'Wwwhhhaaat wwweee're doooiiinnng heeere hhhaaas nnnooot rrreeeaaallly bbbeeen dddefffined yyyettt,' shouted the Time Pig, its words sounding as if each were made of rubber and had been individually stretched.

'Sssccciiieeennntttiiiifffiiicccaaallly dddeeefffined, I mmmeeeaaannn,' it went on. 'Bbbuuuttt sssooommme dddaaayyy sssooommmeee-ooonnne wwwiiilll cccooome aaalllooonnnggg wwwhhhooo wwwiiilll dddeeefffiiine iiittt aaalll. Aaannnddd ttthhhaaattt iiinnndddiiivvviiiddduuuaaalll wwwiiilll ccclllaaaiiimmm ttthhhaaattt I'mmm ooonnnlllly *rrreeelllaaatttiiive!*' The Time Pig gave a hoarse laugh. 'Aaannnddd yyyooouuu kkknnnooowww wwwhhhaaattt? Hhheee'lll bbbeee aaabbbsssooolllluuutely rrriiiggghhhttt!'

The tunnel continually changed shape. It was sometimes circular, sometimes rectangular, sometimes triangular, then circular again, then flat, and so on. In the end, everything around them went as black as the bottom of a well, and they flew on unmoving through the starless darkness—for an eternity, or so it seemed to Gustave.

'I'm sure this seems like an eternity to you,' called the Time Pig, 'but it's less than a hundred years.'

'You mean we're travelling a hundred years into the future?' asked Gustave.

'Not quite, but more or less.'

The Time Pig looked round with an uneasy expression on its rosy face.

'I don't like this dark stretch of the Gully. It's a part of the universe I prefer not to linger in—there are too many riffraff around. But that's how it is with short cuts, they can often be hard going.'

From the depths of the Gully came a sound that seemed familiar to Gustave. He couldn't quite place where he knew it from, but he involuntarily associated it with extreme danger. Although still distant, it seemed to be approaching rapidly.

'Talk of the devil,' groaned the Time Pig. 'Now there'll be trouble.'

At last Gustave managed to identify the source of the sound— or rather, the sources, because they were heading straight towards him with an ever-increasing roar. They were the *Siamese Twins Tornado*, the two telepathic whirlwinds that had sunk his ship

Aventure before disappearing into the sky. Now composed of rotating stardust, cosmic gases and eternal ice, they were tossing meteorites and bits of asteroid around and behaving no less tempestuously up here than they had down on earth.

The Time Pig flapped its wings and made straight for them. 'A Siamese Twins Tornado!' it shouted above the din. 'You have to steer straight through the middle, it's the only way.'

'I wish I'd known that earlier,' sighed Gustave. 'If I had, my journey might have taken quite a different course.'

The whirlwinds piled up on either side of him like monstrous great millstones. Their roar was almost enough to burst his skull, and the cosmic turbulence they produced nearly wrenched him off the back of his mount, but he clung tightly to the Time Pig's bristles and tried to duck beneath the thunderbolts the tornadoes hurled back and forth as a means of communication.

Gustave felt he was being torn apart as he and the Time Pig flew through their electrically charged field of force. A shaft of lightning entered one ear, went screaming through his brain, and emerged from the other. He was compelled to listen to the telepathic messages the tornadoes were exchanging. Incredibly savage and ruthless, they conveyed a blind and frenzied urge to destroy everything in their path. Fragments of rock whistled past Gustave's head and cosmic dust filled his nose and mouth, almost taking his breath away. But at last came a jolt and a sound like a net being ripped apart, and they were out the other side. Still rampaging and hurling thunderbolts around, the tornadoes swiftly receded into the darkness of the Galactic Gully.

'Phew!' said the Time Pig. 'Damn those tornadoes! I told you, this is where the worst riffraff in the universe hang out. Did you know they communicate by thunderbolt?'

'Yes, I did,' said Gustave.

The Time Pig raised its eyebrows. 'You know a great deal.'

They glided along through the silence and darkness for ages, and Gustave began to doubt if this really was a short cut. Where did it lead to, anyway? Into the future, fair enough, but where in the future, exactly? Before he could put that question to the Time Pig, clouds suddenly welled up out of the darkness, and the Galactic Gully resounded with cries, howls and frantic whinnying sounds.

'Not that too!' groaned the Time Pig. 'I hate this part of the cosmos!'

A rider on a wild, snorting charger came galloping towards them. Gustave recognised him at once, although he looked strangely altered. It was Death, wearing his billowing cloak and brandishing a scythe, and following him on foot came a band of rampaging demons. Whether or not he noticed Gustave and his imposing mount, he didn't spare them a glance but galloped past with head erect. It struck Gustave that his face looked less . . . well, less *dead* than before. Once bare bone, his skull seemed now to be thinly covered with skin, although his eye sockets were as black and empty as ever.

The wild horde vanished as suddenly as it had appeared, heading in the same direction as the tornadoes.

'That was Death,' the Time Pig explained.

'I noticed,' Gustave called back. 'But you said he was in his house on the moon.'

'So he is. We're in a Galactic Drainpipe—everything works rather differently up here, my boy. You must bid farewell to your traditional ideas of time, or you'll lose your mind.'

'Why did Death look so young?'

'That's easy: because he still *was* young. That was Death a few hundred years ago, in his storm-and-stress phase. He was probably on his way to afflict humanity with some plague or other.' The Time Pig spat contemptuously into the darkness. 'He was far more ambitious in those days—utterly convinced that his activities were worthwhile and full of bright ideas: epidemics, crusades, wars, massacres, revolutions! But no matter how hard he toiled, the world's population doubled and redoubled in spite of him. At some stage he simply ran out of steam.' The Time Pig gave a sympathetic laugh. 'He used to have many more hangers-on, as you saw, but look at him today! Just a skeleton—a mere shadow of his former self. He does his job by the book and skulks in his retirement home on the moon. Little boys are all he frightens nowadays. His sole companion these days is his crazy sister. Death has become an old-age pensioner.'

'So Death is growing older too?'

'Of course,' said the Time Pig. 'Even *I* am growing older, damn it, and I'm time itself! Nobody can escape that fate. Anyone who doesn't like it must find himself another universe.'

Gustave once more heard the sound that had greeted him when they entered the Galactic Gully: the sound of rapids gurgling over boulders. It quickly swelled and became a roar. The darkness paled, the tunnel transformed itself once more into an immense, multicoloured shaft filled with whirling specks of red, yellow and blue light.

'We're nearly there!' yelled the Time Pig. 'Hang on tight!'

Crunching, crackling sounds rang out once more inside Gustave's head, and all at once he and his mount were catapulted back into the darkness of space. All movement ceased. The black void was cold, silent, and filled with stars.

'First floor,' the Time Pig announced solemnly. 'The future.'

To Gustave the future looked just like the present: a black void with white holes in it.

'I know how you're feeling now,' said the Time Pig. 'You're disappointed.'

Gustave nodded.

'You pictured the future differently, didn't you, but up here almost nothing changes—not dramatically, at any rate. You see that mist over there?'

'That cloud of gas? The one that looks like a horse's head?' Gustave couldn't help thinking of Pancho again.

'Precisely. It'll look just the same a hundred million years from now, yet it's changing all the time, every second.'

'Why does it look like a horse's head?'

'No idea. Why does a horse's head look like a horse's head? Why do I look like a pig? Why do you look the way you do? I don't think there's any deeper significance in it.'

Suddenly, music could be heard—beautiful, ghostly music such as Gustave had heard once before: it was the song of the seahorses. A fleet of jellyfish sailed past. Yellow, red and orange, they kept time to the music like ballet dancers.

'What are the jellyfish doing here?' asked Gustave, who thought he recognised one of them. It had a red body and was trailing some yellow tentacles behind it.

'Those are the *Last Jellyfish*. They're cosmic mourners, so to speak. They slosh around up here until someone drowns down on earth. The jellyfish appear to those who meet their death by drowning.'

Gustave now caught sight of some more creatures: feverishly fluttering hummingbirds, clouds of multicoloured butterflies with wings the size of open newspapers, flamingos, deep-sea fish, stingrays, and huge dragonflies whose chitinous bodies glittered like polished semi-precious stones.

'Depending on the way you die,' the Time Pig went on, 'you see one of the *Last Creatures*. The *Last Butterflies* appear to people who burn to death, the *Last Hummingbirds* to victims of heart attacks. There's a regular menagerie up here.'

An armada of octopuses floated elegantly past. Snakes with yellow and green stripes wriggled weightlessly through the void. Pink flamingos strutted along with military precision.

'The less painful the death, the less attractive the creature you see. If you die peacefully of old age, all you see is a chicken—the *Last Chicken*. It clucks, and you're a goner.'

'Is it true that Death gets your soul afterwards,' asked Gustave, 'and tosses it into the sun to keep it burning?'

'You mean you know the great mystery of the universe?' said the Time Pig. 'You never cease to surprise me, my boy.'

Gustave gave a modest little cough. 'Death told me by mistake.'

'Of course he told you, but not by mistake. He broadcasts it far and wide—he tells everyone, whether or not they want to hear it.'

The Time Pig flapped its wings, and the creatures disappeared from Gustave's field of vision.

'But to revert to your question: I've no idea whether such things as souls exist. Death makes a big fuss about them, but nobody knows what he really puts in those coffins of his. It may be souls, but it may be just hot air. The sun goes on burning come what may—it was burning before there was any life or death in the solar system. Know what I think?'

'No.'

The Time Pig glanced round furtively, as if afraid of being overheard, then lowered its voice to a conspiratorial whisper. 'I think the whole thing's a monumental hoax. I think Death kicks up this fuss just to distract attention from the futility of what he does.'

'So there aren't any souls at all!'

The Time Pig raised its voice again. 'I didn't say that. I've no idea, as I already said. I'm pig ignorant, that's all.' It stopped flapping its wings. 'We're there!'

Gustave couldn't see a thing, just cosmic darkness strewn with twinkling stars.

'Look beneath us!' said the Time Pig, and turned so that Gustave could see past its head into the depths below. He felt dizzy. Beneath them yawned a shaft perhaps three hundred feet in diameter, a seemingly endless tunnel suffused with green light.

'Hold on tight!' called the Time Pig. 'We're now entering the cosmic records department!'

Folding its wings, it plummeted downwards, and they plunged into the luminous shaft like a stone falling down a well. Gustave now saw that the shaft possessed a geometrical structure, a framework of vertical and horizontal lines that created a pattern reminiscent of a filing cabinet.

He even thought he made out some drawers, and each drawer bore the letter A.

'This is the *Corridor of Possibilities*,' the Time Pig called as they continued their nosedive. 'It's where the cosmic bureaucrats try to instil some order into cosmic chaos. They fail, of course, just as they do in real life. They try to get control of things and classify them—file them away in drawers. They try to assemble all the possibilities in the universe and file them alphabetically. An absurd idea, naturally, but that's bureaucrats for you.' The Time Pig gave a contemptuous grunt. 'Can you imagine how many possibilities the universe has to offer? No, you can't. That's why this shaft is so deep—unimaginably deep. We could go on falling for another few million light years, and we'd still be at letter A. Whoops! We've reached the honeycombs!'

Branching off the shaft was a horizontal passage filled with blue light. The Time Pig gave its right wing a vigorous flap, and they turned off along it.

Set in the immensely high walls on either side of them were vast numbers of superimposed and juxtaposed cells like those in a honeycomb. Some were triangular, others four- or five-sided, and each contained a living creature. There were men and women in the most diverse forms of dress: trousers, gowns, suits of armour and curious garments Gustave had never seen before. But there were also birds, bears, cats, dogs, fish, tigers, chamois, cows, ducks, chickens, armadillos, crocodiles, zebras, snakes, seals, rats—one creature to each cell. Many cells seemed to be completely deserted, but closer inspection enabled Gustave to make out an insect buzzing around or a shellfish clinging to the wall. In one cell, a solitary (three-headed) ant was crawling across the floor. Gustave saw many unfamiliar creatures with two, three, four, five, or even more heads. Some consisted of silver light threaded with pulsating blue veins, others had dozens of tentacles and glowing red eyes. Gustave saw flickering creatures made of gas and a bird made of water. *Were* they animals at all?

'Well, there it is,' said the Time Pig, slowing down, 'the *Future Contingency Honeycomb*. It contains all the existences in the universe, neatly sorted out and filed away. All these living creatures have something in common. Have you noticed it, by any chance?'

Gustave looked round. They glided past another few hundred cells while he pondered the question.

'Hm. Where the people and some of the animals are concerned, it strikes me they're all very old.'

'Very observant of you,' said the Time Pig. 'Now look carefully.'

It flew over to a cell in which an elderly man was sitting and hovered right in front of it.

'Hey,' said Gustave, 'why do we have to look at this poor old geriatric? I'd sooner examine a few of these extraterrestrial life forms. They *are* extraterrestrials, aren't they? Creatures from other planets? Later on I could draw them for scientists and—'

'Hey!' the Time Pig broke in. 'Your task, remember?'

'What do you mean?'

'You're supposed to meet yourself, aren't you? All right, then: that old man is *you*!'

Gustave was instantly fascinated by the sight of the old man. He studied every little detail of the cell and its occupant, as he always did in the case of objects he intended to draw.

The man was sitting in a high-backed wing chair. Gustave couldn't tell how old he was. Seventy or eighty, perhaps, but he could have been a hundred. Hale and hearty-looking despite his gaunt frame, he was brandishing a slender sword in the air and vigorously stamping his feet as he read aloud from a book. Most surprising of all, Gustave could actually *see* what the old man was

reading about: *the whole room was filled with adventures*—he couldn't have described it any other way.

Kneeling at the man's feet was a pretty young woman—from a well-to-do family, to judge by her clothes—who was being chained up by a brutal fiend with a knife between his teeth. One remarkable feature of the scene was the relative size of the figures: the young woman and her captor were less than half as big as the old man.

The room was teeming with even smaller figures, some of them really tiny. Jousting on the floor were two knights so small that they could comfortably have ridden on mice. A dragon the size of a domestic cat had crawled beneath the wing chair and was dismembering a big book with its claws.

Elsewhere in the room, a dozen or more knights and soldiers equipped with horses and long lances were engaged in a murderous battle. Gustave even made out a gryphon flying through the air with a maiden on its back. In the left foreground lay a giant's head which had been hacked off and held up by the hair. The face bore a surprising resemblance to that of the giant named Emashtimact or Mathematics.

The old man remained unaffected by all the commotion around him. He continued to read aloud, defiantly brandishing his sword.

'Yes,' said the Time Pig, 'that old man is you—more precisely, you in eighty years' time. He's ninety-two. Almost incredible, eh?'

'Will I really live that long?'

'That remains to be seen. You're looking at your *spatio-temporal continuum projection*—your goal, but not necessarily your destination. It all depends how well you make out against disease, war, accidents, et cetera. Against death, in other words. But ninety-two? Pretty unlikely, with someone as ambitious as you. In your case I'd predict a heart attack in the fifties. A good way to die, incidentally. You're there one moment and gone the next.'

'But how can I be sitting there if I *don't* live that long?'

'Every living creature possesses a spatio-temporal continuum projection. Why? For, er, statistical reasons—something like that. The projections show every living creature in the universe at its maximum possible age. Don't ask me how the system works. I don't have to bother about all that stuff; it's cosmic bureaucracy and accountancy, that's all. Luckily, I deal with other problems.'

The Time Pig heaved a sigh of relief before continuing.

'What I wanted to show you was this. You see that man, don't you? He's you. Or he could have been you. Or *he* certainly was *you*, but it isn't certain that *you* will some time be *him*. Er . . . ' The pig broke off. 'Now I've gone and lost my thread.' It screwed up its eyes and peered at the cell once more. 'Ah, yes,' it went on. 'We've no idea whether the old man is happy or discontented. Perhaps the creatures around him are all the figures you'll devise during your lifetime as an artist, and they're keeping you company—dispelling the loneliness of old age. Perhaps that's what the projection is telling us.'

The pig gave a little cough.

'Alternatively, a less attractive possibility: the old man has lost his marbles. Senile dementia, perhaps, or the effect of a flower pot falling on his head in the prime of life, or . . . How do I know? And now he's sitting there in the loony-bin, surrounded by ghosts. Perhaps they're hallucinations induced by a burst blood vessel in the brain, or by excessive indulgence in alcohol. Make the most of every moment—perhaps he took that advice too literally! In that case, a heart attack at fifty might be preferable. Know what I mean?'

'No,' said Gustave.

The Time Pig gave a strenuous grunt.

'How can I explain it to you? I'm not saying life makes no sense, not exactly. It's just that there's . . . that it's, er . . . '

'Pointless?' Gustave suggested.

The Time Pig looked dumbfounded. 'Got it in one! You really do know an amazing amount for your age.'

'But why can't we all grow as old as we look in our honeycomb cells?' asked Gustave.

The Time Pig groaned as if it were beginning to find Gustave's weight on its back too much of a strain. 'Don't ask *me* that. You must ask the Second Most Monstrous of All Monsters.'

'The one called Anxiety, you mean?'

'No, Anxiety is only the Third Most Monstrous of All Monsters. The Second Most Monstrous of All Monsters is *Fate*.'

Gustave strove to memorise this.

'Oh, by the way,' exclaimed the Time Pig. 'While we're on the subject, the Knight-Eating Giant Saurian of Lake Blue-Blood is just a show-off. It only comes 175th in the Most Monstrous Monster world rankings.'

The Time Pig uttered another rather uneasy grunt, and Gustave thought he detected a faint note of impatience in its next words.

'Life, my boy, is more than just an enjoyable, adventurous journey. It also means watching Death at work, and that's the hardest thing of all. You have to be able to endure the sight. Are you prepared to do that?'

'I think so.'

'I didn't expect any other answer. Everyone says that at first.' The Time Pig looked suddenly serious, almost solemn. 'Right, so you're ready to tackle life and all its surprises?'

'Yes,' said Gustave, although this time he wasn't sure what the pig was getting at.

'Excellent,' said the pig, spreading its wings. 'In that case, I've got a genuine surprise for you right now.' It flapped its leathery pinions, and in an instant they were once more speeding along the tunnel past billions of honeycomb cells filled with the projections of ageing existences. Gustave would have liked to take a closer look at one or two octopus-like extraterrestrials, but the tunnel seemed to grow steadily higher and wider and the cells further and further away, until he and the Time Pig were once more out in space with a thousand distant suns crackling around them.

The Time Pig came to a halt. Floating immediately below them was a balloon resembling a soap bubble little bigger than a wine cask. The pig instructed Gustave to climb down on to it, and he obeyed without hesitation, eager for another lesson in cosmology.

'I'm giving you your own solar system,' the Time Pig said generously. 'Make the most of it. That gas bubble contains all the necessary chemical elements. With a bit of luck, it'll develop into a genuine sun complete with its own planets and all the trimmings. You'll have to be patient, that's all. It'll only take a few hundred billion years or so.'

Gustave was flabbergasted. 'You mean you're leaving me here? Can't you simply fly me to the moon? I still have one last task to perform.'

'Now don't get fresh with me!' the Time Pig said reprovingly. 'From here to the moon is—wait a minute—7,679,781,887,964,997,865,457 parsecs. It would take me four hundred billion years, even at my maximum cruising speed, and that's far too long. I've already sacrificed whole regiments of microseconds for your benefit.'

'But what about the Galactic Gully? Couldn't we take a short cut?'

'The Galactic Gully only takes one-way traffic. Didn't I mention that?'

Gustave stamped his foot furiously, and the gas bubble quivered. 'No, you didn't!'

'Oh, then I must have forgotten to.' The Time Pig shrugged its shoulders apologetically. 'Nothing to be done, I'm afraid.'

'But I'll starve to death here,' Gustave protested. 'I'll die if you maroon me here.'

'Yes, but it doesn't matter,' the Time Pig declared, raising one clawed foot. 'Your components will dissolve into gas and form the basis of new life. That's how your own solar system came into being, by the way. I showed the honeycomb cells to a little boy from a planet in the Andromeda constellation, gave him a lecture on life and the universe, and put him down on a gas bubble. That bubble developed into the earth and all its human and animal inhabitants—yourself included. Such is the life cycle! That's how inhabited solar systems originate: you deposit little boys on gas bubbles. It's the greatest cosmic miracle of all: little beginnings, big results!'

The Time Pig slowly ascended, its wings whirring like a hummingbird's. 'So, now I really must be going,' it called to

Gustave. 'The universe freezes if I remain in the same spot for too long, and I'm sure you wouldn't like to take the responsibility for that, would you?' It flapped its wings and soared off across an ocean of sparkling suns. Just before reaching a constellation whose outlines bore a remarkable resemblance to a pig, it turned left and disappeared into the black cosmic void.

Once Gustave had finally settled down on the iridescent gas bubble that would one day become his solar system, and once he had taken stock of his new place in the universe, he experienced a sensation he hadn't enjoyed for a long time: a feeling of serenity.

He had been permanently on the move and constantly involved in new adventures since . . . yes, since when, exactly? To be precise, ever since he'd put to sea aboard the *Aventure*. He hadn't had a moment's peace of mind from then on, what with the Siamese Twins Tornado, the terrible fate of Dante and his other seamen, Death and his demented sister, their wager on his soul, his aerial flight astride the gryphon, the dragon-juice factory and the naked Amazons, his duel with the dragon, the Last Jellyfish, the beautiful damsel (*a cold stab in the heart*), the empty suit of armour, his encounters with Pancho and the mysterious dream princess, and Pancho's entombment in the forest of evil spirits. After that, his swigs of Wanderlust Wine had speeded everything up. Then had come the Valley of the Monsters, his conversation with Anxiety, his battle with the Terrible Titans, Lake Blue-Blood and the Knight-Eating Giant Saurian, and, finally, his encounter with the Most Monstrous of All Monsters.

He had flown past the moon through space and time, traversed a Galactic Gully, seen Death at work, escaped the Siamese Twins Tornado for a second time, and been privileged to see the *Last Creatures* and the Horse-Head Nebula. He had inspected the cosmic records department and the future-contingency honey-comb with its spatio-temporal continuum projections. Last but not least, he had met himself and been presented with a solar system of his own. Not bad for a single night's journey!

Having reviewed all these happenings in his mind's eye, he leant back and surveyed the boundless space around him. Just then he felt another stab in the heart. He clutched his chest in alarm, but it was less like a stitch than a warm, therapeutic feeling. It came again, and again, and again. His broken heart was healing!

'A broken heart sewn up with four stitches,' he told himself. 'They're bound to leave a scar, but the extent of my present problems is such that I may as well forget about the past—and the future, too! So much for naked damsels! I'd better resign myself at once to dying here. At least I'm so far away from Death, he won't get my soul—if I've got one.'

With a sigh, Gustave lay back and looked up at the stars. It was quite comfortable, lying on the gas bubble, which felt like a bag filled with lukewarm water. Millions of suns were shining overhead, but the sight was already beginning to bore him.

'That spatio-temporal continuum projection was way off target,' he said, projecting the words into space. 'Under present circumstances, I've about as much chance of living till I'm ninety-two as of meeting up with a few old friends out here. Or of being hit by a comet.' He heaved another sigh and started to count stars to pass the time. One of them looked different from the others. It was duller than the rest, and it was moving. No, it wasn't twinkling, and it seemed to be getting bigger. Either that, or it was approaching at high speed. Gustave could also hear a noise that seemed to be growing steadily louder. It sounded like the thunder of hoofs, but Gustave surmised that it was the popping of gas bubbles in a comet's tail.

'It's a comet!' he murmured. 'Of course it is, and it's heading straight for me! That's great! I get my own solar system, and the first thing that happens is, I'm smashed to smithereens by a cosmic iceberg!'

But the nearer the object came, the more certain he became that it *wasn't* a comet. At first he thought it might be Death and his wild cavalcade, because he heard neighing sounds and the hoofbeats grew louder. He even thought he made out a horse, but then he saw that it was a whole team of horses. More precisely, it was an ancient chariot drawn by four chargers and leaving a fiery trail swathed in dense smoke. The horses were galloping along on the flames and flapping their wings, because they all had wings like angels.

'Great,' Gustave said to himself. 'They're probably the *Last Horses* you see before dying of starvation in space. All that's missing is a little background music.'

All at once he recognised Pancho Sansa among the horses. But Pancho was not the only familiar member of this extraordinary ensemble, for the driver of the cosmic chariot was none other than his trusty Dante, boatswain of the *Aventure*.

Whinnying, snorting and scattering sparks, the team came to a halt beside Gustave and his gas bubble. He stood up, precariously balancing on its thin outer skin.

At first all three were too taken aback to open the conversation. They scratched their heads, opened their mouths and closed them again, and Pancho gave an inarticulate snort. Then Dante broke the silence.

'What are you doing out here in space, Cap'n? I thought you'd been torn to pieces by the Siamese Twins Tornado.'

'And I thought you'd jumped into Lake Blue-Blood and been devoured by the Most Monstrous of All Monsters,' Pancho chimed in, not without a hint of reproach in his voice.

'I might ask you two the same question,' Gustave retorted. 'In my case the answers are two long stories. First, though, tell me how *you* both got here. Perhaps your stories are shorter.'

'Aye-aye, Cap'n!' Dante saluted smartly. 'Shall I go first?'

Pancho and Gustave nodded.

'Well,' Dante began, 'I was sucked up into space with the rest of the crew, wasn't I? All those good seamen were scattered to the four winds, which was a shame—except for the cabin boy, who was an idle landlubber and got what he deserved.'

Dante spat into the void.

'So there I was, floating around in space with the blue earth and its seas below me and the stars above, and I thought: Hey, this isn't such a bad way to die. After all, I've spent most of my life like this— in closer contact with the water, but that's all. So I was floating around, waiting to die, when I heard a sudden roar—surprising how well you can hear in space, isn't it?—and who should come flying along but *Death*, the silly ass. He had a funny-looking old woman with him—his sister, it turned out later. She gave me a really nasty look, and he asked me who I was, as I knew he would, because that's always the first question Death asks, isn't it? I wondered whether to fool him by giving a false name—the cabin boy's, for instance—but then I thought: What the hell, let him take me. Better that than floating around here for ever, and he'll nab me sooner or later, so I said:

'"Dante."

'"Dante, the famous poet?" says he.

'"No," say I, "Dante the unfamous boatswain."

'"What's a boatswain doing up here in space?" says he. So I told him the story of the *Aventure* and the Siamese Twins Tornado, and when I mentioned your name he started to laugh. "You're in luck, Boatswain Dante," says he, "because I now see a chance to kill two birds with one stone. Would you like to become a *soul-coffin transporter*?"'

Gustave gave an involuntary gasp.

'I said yes, naturally. I mean, better a regular job of any kind than dead. So that's what I do now: I haul soul-coffins from the moon to the sun and stoke it with them, because business is booming and Death has got tired of doing all the work himself. I have my own wagon and the prospect of immortality if I get through a trial period of ten thousand years. Well, Cap'n, that's my story: I've become a servant of Death.'

Dante saluted again. Gustave drew a deep breath. 'And what's your story, Pancho?'

The horse cleared its throat.

'Well, I fell into the crocodile's jaws and the monster swallowed me whole, as you saw. But then the stupid creature dived, and water came pouring into its mouth. So I wasn't just devoured, I drowned as well. I died: end of story.' Pancho grinned.

'Come on,' said Gustave, 'don't keep us in suspense.'

'All right,' Pancho went on. 'So I died. But I really wasn't done yet, believe me. I still had *something* in mind, but that's how it is: you have to take things as they come. I couldn't wait to find out what would happen next, of course. Was there a horses' heaven? Would I end up in a horses' hell? Would I go out in a blaze of white light, or what?'

'Get to the point, Pancho!'

'Well, I really did enter a blaze of white light. I went trotting in, and all at once I saw a jellyfish—a beautiful jellyfish—and heard music—beautiful music—and I thought I'd gone mad, and the jellyfish started to speak, and it said—'

'No need to elaborate, I know that jellyfish.'

'You know it? Did you drown too, then?'

'Not exactly. Go on.'

'Very well, so I went to heaven, for how can I put it? *There really is a horses' heaven!* I've even got wings—I've become an equine angel, so to speak. Great, isn't it? I'd never have thought horses rated so highly up here, but there are whole constellations named after them! There's even a huge nebula shaped like a horse's head, did you know?'

'Yes,' said Gustave, 'I did.'

Pancho looked astonished. 'You know plenty!'

'I've been around a lot lately,' Gustave explained. 'But how come you know Dante?'

'Oh, that was pure chance. A place in his team fell vacant. I saw his advert on the blackboard, and—'

'What blackboard?'

'The cosmic blackboard, of course. We've got everything up here, you know. Blackboards, black holes, galactic gullies—'

'Yes, yes,' Gustave broke in. 'So you've become a servant of Death too.'

'Not quite,' said Pancho. 'We made a deal. Each of us can

terminate my contract of employment at a million years' notice.' He bared his equine teeth in a broad grin.

'But what brings you to this remote part of the universe?'

'Oh, I was giving the horses a bit of exercise, Cap'n,' said Dante. 'All we normally do is the short-haul flight between the sun and the moon, which gets boring after a while. We like to look at other galaxies during the lunch break.'

A miniature comet zoomed over their heads, hissing and crackling like a sparkler. Gustave drew another deep breath before he put his last question. 'You wouldn't by any chance be on your way to the moon to collect some more soul-coffins, would you?'

'Yes, we are!' Pancho exclaimed. 'How did you know?'

'I'm good at guessing games, you know that,' said Gustave. 'Remember the giants?'

'That was the tops, that business with the giants!' Pancho said reminiscently.

'A little too gory for my taste, but they started it. Would you mind if I came too? I've got an appointment with Death.'

'Of course, Cap'n,' cried Dante. 'Get in and we'll take you to the moon, that goes without saying.'

Gustave boarded the chariot and took his place beside Dante. He was about to give the order to set off, if only from force of habit, when something occurred to him. 'But how can we get to the moon before daybreak? The Time Pig calculated that it would take several billion years.'

'Oh, the Time Pig,' Pancho said derisively. '*That* fat hog with his mouse's wings! *Our* wings are in the Pegasus class, my friend, and the chariot wheels are made of compressed comet dust. As for the suspension—'

'That's enough, Pancho!' cried Dante. He tugged at the reins and Pancho relapsed into silence.

'I could tell you my story during the flight,' Gustave suggested. 'It'll pass the time.'

'No need, Cap'n. This contraption is rather different from a sailing ship. Hold on tight, won't you?'

Gustave gripped the seat cushions tight.

'Gee-up!' cried Dante, shaking the reins. There was a whirring sound as the horses flapped their wings. The chariot set off with a jerk, throwing Gustave back into his seat.

'Whoa!' cried Dante. 'We're there.'

Gustave had barely had time to blink. He leant over the side of the chariot and looked down, almost unable to believe his eyes. Floating beneath him was the moon, a big white sphere sprinkled with craters. Further away he could see the earth with its blue seas, and much further away the blazing, dazzling sun. They really were back home in their own solar system.

'Phew,' he said in astonishment, 'that was quick.'

'Yes,' said Dante, 'we've got all the most modern technological equipment here. We need it, the way demand keeps on growing.'

They came in to land, and the chariot touched down gently in a crater.

'The Sea of Tranquillity, Cap'n—end of the line. That's Death's house straight ahead.' Dante jerked his head at a gloomy, two-storeyed building on the edge of the crater. There was a light on upstairs. The tall double doors, which were shut, had a bust over the

lintel. 'Strange,' thought Gustave. 'Why do those doors seem so familiar?'

A big raven was circling above the sinister building, its hoarse cries reverberating around the walls of the crater.

'There's a light on,' Dante remarked, 'so they must be at home. They could also be fluttering around somewhere—they do that every night—but they can't be far away.'

Gustave eyed the raven with surprise. 'So there are birds on the moon?'

'Yes, Death brought a few earth creatures with him to make the place seem more homely. There are ravens, owls, rats, bats and spiders. And worms, lots of worms. Ants too, of course, but they were here already.'

'What do you think of Death—as an employer, I mean?' Gustave asked as he dismounted from the chariot. The surface was as soft and yielding as rubber.

'I honestly can't complain. I mean, he's not the type of person you'd care to go on vacation with, but we don't have much to do with each other in any case. His sister fills the soul-coffins with fresh souls inside the house, so they say. He stacks them in the backyard and I collect them, that's all. He and his crazy sister squabble a lot indoors—I sometimes hear them at it.'

Dante looked up, distracted by a fluttering sound too loud to be made by ravens.

'Oh, here he comes,' he said in a subdued voice. 'Your appointment. We'd better get on with our work right away. The boss doesn't like his employees dilly-dallying.'

Gustave followed Dante's gaze. Death and his sister, both attired in billowing robes, were coming in to land. Death, who was clasping Dementia tightly in his arms, had reassumed the skeletal appearance Gustave remembered from their first encounter.

'So long, partner,' Pancho called hurriedly. 'It was an honour to ride with you.' And he put out his right forehoof.

'Mind how you go in that crazy contraption of yours,' said Gustave.

'Don't worry,' Pancho replied. 'I told you: *If Death supplies you with something, he quality-controls it himself.*'

Dante cracked his whip, the horses flapped their wings, and the chariot took off.

'Oh yes,' Pancho called from above, 'one more thing.'

Gustave looked up at him.

'That business with the stupid crocodile—it's just between the two of us, right?'

'Right!' Gustave called back, waving goodbye.

The chariot quickly gained height. Gustave heard Dante ask a question in the distance—'What was that you said about a crocodile?'—and then it disappeared among the twinkling stars.

At that moment the weird pair made a silent landing on the surface of the moon. Dementia stepped aside as soon as her brother released her. Sitting down on the soft ground, she started singing to herself and playing with moon pebbles. Death turned his pale face in Gustave's direction. Up here in the cold light of space he looked even more unreal than he had on earth. His tone was cold and businesslike.

'You've performed all your tasks to date, I hear. Do you have the tooth?'

'Yes,' Gustave replied diplomatically, without producing his trophy. 'I do.'

'Then hand it over!' The skeleton's voice betrayed a mixture of impatience and greed.

'Not so fast,' said Gustave. 'What do you plan to do with it?'

'None of your business!'

Dementia giggled. 'He wants to kill himself with it!'

'*Dementia!*' snarled Death.

'The Time Pig's tooth is the only weapon Death can commit suicide with,' Dementia continued implacably. 'You've no idea how badly he wants it!'

'Just a minute,' said Gustave. 'Death longs for death? Are you saying that, if he kills himself with the Time Pig's tooth, no one else will have to die?'

'That's it.' Dementia giggled again. 'Before long, thanks to you, there won't be any more funerals. You're a regular hero, my lad.'

Gustave produced the tooth from his breastplate and handed it to Death, who eagerly snatched it from him, then held it up and examined it at length in the moonlight.

'Well, go on,' cried Dementia. 'Kill yourself!'

Death lowered the tooth.

'It's the wrong one,' he sighed. 'It should have been an incisor. This is a molar.'

Dementia rounded on Gustave. 'The wrong tooth!' she jeered. 'You got the wrong tooth!' And she threw a moon pebble at him.

'Then you haven't completed your tasks after all,' the skeleton said grimly.

'How was I to know?' Gustave protested angrily. 'I've brought you a tooth from the Most Monstrous of All Monsters. That was the task you set me. You never said anything about an incisor.'

Dementia backed him up. 'I'm afraid the boy's right, brother dear. It's your own fault for not being more specific.'

'Very well,' Death said sulkily, 'but he still hasn't completed all his tasks. There's still one to go.'

'I know,' said Gustave, 'that's why I'm here. I'm waiting.'

'Right,' Death murmured, 'your last task . . . er, your last task . . . '

'Well?' Dementia cut in.

'Er . . . your last task, er . . . Tell me, my boy, what do you want to be when you grow up? *If* you survive, that is.'

'I want to be an artist,' Gustave replied firmly. 'I want to draw and paint.'

'I see,' said Death. 'So you want to be an artist, eh? Good, then this will be your final task: You're to make a portrait of me. Depending on how it turns out, I shall decide whether or not you've performed the task satisfactorily.'

Death clicked his fingers, and Gustave suddenly found himself holding a sheet of paper and a silver pencil.

He examined the paper. It was of excellent quality—rough, heavy cartridge paper—and the pencil fitted his hand like a glove. He couldn't have wished for a better task. If there was one thing he was good at, it was drawing. He sat down on a big white moonstone and got started.

Gustave drew as if his life depended on it—which it did. He made his drawing an allegorical composition: the Grim Reaper seated on a globe with a scythe and an hourglass in his bony hands.

He had never drawn better in all his days. Proportions, hatching, shadows, drapery, the anatomical depiction of the skull—all were handled with absolute perfection. Gustave had always longed to be able to draw like that: so quickly, so unerringly, so *printably*! Yes indeed, the drawing was fit to be printed as it stood; there was no need to make a woodcut or etching of it. It was the best piece of work he had ever produced.

'Finished?' Death asked impatiently. 'Give it here!'

Gustave handed him the sheet of paper. Death submitted it to long and careful scrutiny. Then he cleared his throat.

'This is the lousiest drawing ever! Nothing's the way it should be! The proportions are all wrong, the hatching's amateurish, the drapery's an utter flop. The chiaroscuro effects are, er, totally lacking in subtlety. You can't even handle perspective properly, and you've botched the outlines. As for the anatomical depiction of the skull, I've never looked like that in my life!'

Gustave was shattered. It was the most scathing verdict that had ever been passed on a drawing of his.

'And what about the golden mean?' Death pursued. 'All good drawings have to be composed in accordance with the golden mean. I can see no sign of it.'

Gustave knitted his brow. *Golden mean? What was he talking about? Did he mean the golden section? Hey, just a minute—did Death have the first idea about drawing?*

'And the paint!' Death sneered. 'Far too thickly applied.'

Dementia uttered a shrill laugh.

The paint? thought Gustave. *What paint? It's a black-and-white drawing!*

Death tossed the sheet of paper aside. 'No good at all,' he said, turning his empty eye sockets in Gustave's direction.

Of course! Gustave thought suddenly. At that moment everything became clear to him. *His eyes! Death doesn't have any: he's blind!*

Dementia tittered.

So be it, Gustave said to himself. *He's fooled me after all. It wouldn't have mattered how good the drawing was, he'd have rejected it on principle.*

'Does that mean I've failed the final test?' he asked coldly.

'No,' Death replied. 'It wasn't a question of passing or failing. What matters is whether you're *prepared to die.*'

The skeletal figure prepared to deliver a longish lecture.

'I strongly dislike taking a human life while it's still immature. It's much more fun when people are fully developed and at the peak of their abilities. I prefer summoning them to me when they've achieved something—hence all the heart attacks they suffer from fifty onwards.'

Death cackled spitefully.

'Just when they're standing there crowned with success, out of breath after toiling away for years on end—just when they're looking forward to enjoying the fruits of their labours at last— wham, bang! Carrying them off at that stage is the greatest fun of all!' Death punched a couple of holes in space with his bony fists. 'A soul has to be fat. Fat souls burn better, brighter, longer. *Your* soul is a scrawny little thing. Transporting it to the sun wouldn't be worth the effort.'

Death made a dismissive gesture. 'Go away and strive, work, struggle, fail, succeed, fail, and start again from scratch. That way, your soul will swell up like pâté de foie gras. And don't extol life before it's over, because dying is the purpose of existence. But you aren't ready to die, not yet. *You've got to put in a lot more practice first.*'

Death turned away. 'You can go,' he told Gustave curtly, and strode off towards the house, trailing his cloak behind him. Dementia, giggling like a little girl, got up and skipped along in his wake.

'Go? Where to?' Gustave called after them. 'We're on the moon. How can I leave here?'

The sinister siblings paused and turned.

'Oh, yes,' Death growled, 'you mortals still can't fly yet. I keep forgetting that.'

He rummaged in the folds of his robe.

'Here, take these,' he said, producing a pair of leathery wings and holding them out. They looked as if he had removed them from an outsize bat. Gustave went over, took them, and thanked him.

'I designed them myself. I even wear them occasionally, just for show. Strap them on, take up your position on the edge of the crater, and push off. The rest will come by itself.'

Death turned away again. Dementia emitted a silly giggle and hurried after him. Outside the front door, Death paused once more and rummaged in his robe for a considerable time. Gustave heard muffled cursing. 'Ah, here it is!' the skeleton exclaimed at last, triumphantly holding a key aloft.

The big raven landed on the roof just as Death went inside. Dementia slipped in after him, but before the door closed behind her she suddenly paused and looked back at Gustave through the crack, smiling.

Gustave now knew where he had already seen the door—indeed, the whole scene: on the seabed, when he was on the point of drowning.

'We'll meet again!' Dementia called softly, and blew him a kiss. Then she shut the door.

Gustave scaled the highest pinnacle overlooking the Sea of Tranquillity. He put on the leather wings, performed a few knees-bends, and pushed off. Instantly, he shot upwards like a rocket and headed straight for the earth. 'This is even easier than killing giants,' he thought.

He needed no wings while flying through space; his push-off from the moon was enough to catapult him earthwards like a cannon ball. Then, when he entered the earth's atmosphere, the winds enveloped him in their warm, gentle embrace.

For a while he enjoyed free-falling. He had experienced the most varied forms of transportation during the night, but flying by himself struck him as the pleasantest by far. 'How wonderful,' he thought, 'to soar on the wind like a bird!'

He passed the time, while watching the earth draw nearer, by turning a few aerial somersaults and looping the loop.

Yes, he was right on course. There was Europe with the Italian boot protruding into the Mediterranean and, above and to the left of it, France, his native land. The continent ceased to be a vague shape and became a land mass approaching at breakneck speed.

There was Paris, a grey splodge surrounded by the yellow and green of field and forest! Fantastic! Gustave had always wanted to go to Paris. The grey splodge swiftly expanded into a spider's web of streets, and he could already distinguish individual buildings. 'There's the Seine—I'm going to land plumb in the middle of the city!' he cried exultantly. 'I'd better use my wings now.'

He tried to flap them, but they wouldn't move. 'They're still a bit stiff from the low temperatures in space,' he told himself.

But his further attempts to flap them proved just as futile. They remained absolutely rigid, though the membranes between the bones fluttered in the slipstream. Gustave could now make out individual tiles on the roofs. He tried yet again to flap his wings, but they were immovable—quite useless. He was falling like a stone. '*If Death supplies you with something, he quality-controls it himself!*' Pancho's remark flashed through his mind, and he knew he was doomed to die.

He laughed bitterly. 'So Death cheated me after all,' he told himself. 'He saddled me with a pair of useless wings, and I actually thanked him for them . . .'

Gustave saw a big, cobbled square below him—quite a typical Parisian feature.

'I've become a servant of Death after all!' That was his last thought before he hit the cobblestones.

Gustave awoke. He sat up with a smothered cry, eyes wide with terror, forehead beaded with sweat, moist strands of hair glued to his scalp. Where was he? Was he dead? Around him was a grey void in which a light twinkled somewhere. A star? No, this couldn't be space; he was in a room. There were dark walls on either side of him and a ceiling overhead. Was that a gryphon hovering below the ceiling? Yes, and fluttering beside it was a pig with wings like a bat! A dragon emerged from the darkness, opened its lizard-like jaws and spewed out a stream of orange and blue flames. Was that a damsel riding on its back? A *naked* damsel?

There, two waterspouts took shape in the corner of the room and whirled across the floor, moving in concert. A Siamese Twins Tornado, with the *Aventure* running before it! What was going on here? Shadowy, ghostly creatures were swarming everywhere: a bird hopping along on one leg, croaking hoarsely; a hunchbacked dwarf mounted on a grasshopper and waving its cap; two serpent-like monsters rolling around, locked in mortal combat; a gigantic, long-legged spider strutting along. *The whole room was teeming with adventures!*

Exactly, that was it: he was dead—smashed like an egg on the cobblestones of Paris! And this was his *spatio-temporal, future-contingency honeycomb cell*, filled with memories of his all too brief life. He had just turned twelve. This was as far as he had got.

Then his eyes grew accustomed to the half-light, and he really woke up. Bleary-eyed and breathing heavily, he surveyed his surroundings. The bedroom—*his* bedroom—was still in darkness, but slender sunbeams were already stealing through the crack between the curtains. The room seemed to be the wrong way round. Then Gustave realised that he was lying with his head where his feet should have been. The bed was badly rumpled, the undersheet half wrenched off the mattress and one pillow lying on the floor. It looked as if he'd had a violent pillow fight during the night.

He scrambled up and perched on the edge of the bed. While feeling for his slippers, his bare feet encountered the books he'd been reading the night before, which lay scattered around on the floor: Cervantes' *Don Quixote*, Ariosto's *Orlando Furioso*, and Dante's *Inferno*, together with his textbooks on biology, mathematics, geology, physics, astronomy and philosophy—which reminded him that he hadn't done his homework.

But right on top lay the sketchbook in which he'd been scribbling before he went to sleep. Picking it up, he stared bemusedly at the first drawing. Its subject—Death portrayed as a black-robed skeleton seated on the terrestrial globe—had been inspired by a line of poetry he'd read. The folds of the robe were a complete fiasco, the skeleton was anatomically inaccurate. Gustave tossed the sketchbook on the floor.

'It's an utter failure,' he said softly. 'Death was right: I must put in a lot more practice.' He rubbed his eyes and gave a hearty yawn. Then he got up off the edge of the bed, tottered over to the window, and drew the curtains.

It was broad daylight.

The woodcuts reproduced in this volume are taken from the following works illustrated by Gustave Doré: *The Rime of the Ancient Mariner* by Samuel Taylor Coleridge (pp. 3, 9); *Orlando Furioso* by Lodovico Ariosto (pp. 19, 23, 29, 49, 67, 79, 163); *The Raven* by Edgar Allan Poe (pp. 33, 167, 171); *Don Quixote* by Miguel de Cervantes (pp. 95, 109, 115, 147); *Legend of Croquemitaine* by Ernest l'Épine (p. 85); *Gargantua and Pantagruel* by François Rabelais (p. 123); *Paradise Lost* by John Milton (p. 179); and the *Bible* (pp. 139, 183).

For the benefit of those readers who would like to learn more about Gustave Doré, the following pages bear a chronology of the most important events in his life and a list of his principal works.

Anyone interested in reading an essay by Walter Moers on Gustave Doré and how *A Wild Ride through the Night* came into being should consult our website (www.wilde–reise.de).

Chronology

1832   Gustave Doré born on 6 January at 5 rue de la Nuée-Bleue, to Pierre-Louis-Chistophe Doré and his wife Alexandrine Marie-Anne, née Pluchart.

1837   Doré's talent first attracts attention when, at the age of five, he draws caricatures of his relations and teachers in his exercise books.

1839   He starts to learn several musical instruments, becoming a virtuoso on the violin.

1841   The family moves for professional reasons to Bourg-en-Bresse in the Jura. Doré attends the local collège. His first attempt to illustrate Dante's *Divine Comedy*.

1847   First published work: *Les Travaux d'Hercule*, Aubert, Paris.

1848   First visit to Paris with his parents. Doré makes contact with Charles Philipon, a magazine publisher, who puts him under contract as an illustrator. Death of his father.

1849   Doré's mother moves to Paris.

1851   Publication of his early work, *Les Désagréments d'un voyage d'agrément*. He joins the staff of the magazine *L'Illustration*.

1853   Doré illustrates Lord Byron's *Œuvres complètes*.

1854   He publishes his first major illustrated work, *Gargantua et Pantagruel* by Rabelais, which causes a great stir. The same year sees the publication of *Histoire pittoresque de la Sainte-Russie*, a satirical and stylistically audacious illustrated history of the Crimean War which may safely be classified as one of the most imaginative forerunners of the comic strip.
Doré gains his first successes as a painter.

1855	World Exhibition, Paris.
	Doré illustrates Balzac's *Contes drolatiques*. Together with his Rabelais cycle, this lays the foundations of his international renown as a book illustrator. John Ruskin condemns Balzac's text as shamelessly blasphemous and Doré's illustrations as monstrous and disgusting.
1857	Doré illustrates the Comtesse de Ségur's fairy tales. In the ensuing years he devotes himself to a wide variety of projects, some of a non-literary nature.
1861	Dante's *Inferno* marks the beginning of Doré's grand design: a world library of illustrated works. His artistic output becomes steadily more industrialised, and he tackles more and more assignments simultaneously.
1862	Doré illustrates Charles Perrault's fairy stories and Gottfried August Bürger's *Münchhausen*. Preliminary sketches for *Don Quixote*.
1863	*Don Quixote*, his most successful work to date, appears. Only his *Bible* exceeds it in number of editions printed.
1864	Napoleon III invites Doré to spend ten days at his court.
1866	*Don Quixote* becomes an international bestseller and Doré the highest-paid artist of his day. The *Bible* and Milton's *Paradise Lost* appear with Doré's illustrations. His paintings are less successful. The merciless verdict of one contemporary critic: 'Wallpaper is worth more.'
1867	Doré illustrates La Fontaine's *Fables* and Tennyson's *Idylls of the King*.
1868	Disappointed by the failure of his paintings in France, Doré temporarily emigrates to London, where he triumphs as a

painter and illustrator. Opening of the Doré Gallery at 35 New Bond Street. He illustrates Dante's *Purgatory* and *Paradise* and undertakes numerous excursions through the more disreputable districts of London, sometimes with a police escort, for the purpose of making drawings for a *London* volume based on texts by Blanchard Jerrold.

1870   Fall of the French Empire; Napoleon III captured at Sedan.

1872   Doré has begun to sculpt as well. The *London* volume appears, together with several historical works.

1875   He is received in audience by Queen Victoria. Illustrates *The Rime of the Ancient Mariner* by Samuel Coleridge.

1877   Joseph Michaud's *Histoire des croisades* published with illustrations by Doré.

1878   Preliminary illustrations for *A Thousand and One Nights*.

1879   Publication of Ariosto's *Orlando Furioso*, Doré's last major cycle. He is appointed an officer of the Légion d'honneur.

1880   Death of Jacques Offenbach, one of Doré's closest friends.

1881   Doré's mother dies.

1883   Gustave Doré dies of a heart attack in Paris on 23 January. The same year sees the publication of Edgar Allan Poe's *The Raven*, his last illustrated work.

List of Doré's principal illustrated works (from Henri Leblanc)

1847   *Les Travaux d'Hercule*, Doré
1851   *Ces Chinois de Parisiens*, Album
        Les Désagréments d'un voyage d'agrément, Doré
        Musée comique, Album
        Œuvres illustrées du bibliophile Jacob, Paul Lacroix
        Trois artistes incompris et mécontents, Doré
        Seul au monde, A. Brot
1852   *Tableau de Paris*, Edouard Texier
1853   *Œuvres complètes*, Lord Byron
1854   *Le Médecin du cœur*, A. Brot
        Le Bourreau du roi, A. Brot
        Les Différents publics de Paris, Album
        Histoire pittoresque de la Sainte-Russie, Doré
        La Ménagerie parisienne, Album
        Gargantua et Pantagruel, Rabelais
1855   *Contes drolatiques*, Balzac
        La Chasse au lion, Jules Gérard
        Histoire populaire de la Guerre d'Orient, Abbé Mullois
        Les Chercheurs d'or, J. Sherer
        Voyage aux eaux des Pyrénées, Hippolyte Taine
1856   *La France en Afrique*, B. Gastineau
        Contes d'une vieille fille, Mme de Girardin
        L'Insurrection en Chine, Haussmann
        La Légende du Juif Errant, Pierre Dupont
        Le Chevalier Jaufre, Mary Lafon
        L'Habitation au désert, Mayne-Reid

Histoire populaire de France, various authors

Histoire de la Guerre de Mexique, La Bédollière

Contes et légendes, de Laujon

Histoire de la Capitaine Castagnette, L'Épine

Contes, Perrault

La Mythologie du Rhin, X. B. Saintine

1863   *Don Quixote*, Cervantes

Atala, Chateaubriand

Paris illustré, Adolphe Joanne

Bade et la Forêt-Noire, Adolphe Joanne

La Légende de Croque-Mitaine, L'Épine

Sous la tente, Charles Yriarte

1864   *Histoires d'une minute*, Adrien Marx

Histoires des chevaliers, Elizé de Montagnac

1865   *Balle-Franche*, Gustave Aiward

Crécy et Poitiers, J. G. Edgar

The Fairy Realm, Tom Hood

De Paris en Afrique, B. Gastineau

Les Mille et une nuits, Galland

L'Epicuréen, Thomas Moore

La Flêche d'or, M.V. Victor

1866   *Le Capitaine Fracasse*, Théophile Gautier

Paradise Lost, John Milton

La Sainte Bible selon la Vulgate

1867   *The Pyrenees*, H. Blackburn

Toilers of the Sea, Victor Hugo

La France et la Prusse, La Bédollière

Fables, La Fontaine

	River Legends, Knatchbull
1876	*Londres*, L. Enault
	Le Chevalier noir, Mary Lafon
	L'Art en Alsace Lorraine, René Menard
1877	*Histoire de paysans*, Eugène Bonnemère
	Nos petits rois, H. Jousselin
	Histoire des croisades, J. Michaud
	Montreux guide, Rambert
1878	*L'Espagne*, Edmondo de Amicis
	Voyage autour du monde, Comte de Beauvoir
	Voyage aux pays annexés, Victor Duruy
1879	*Le Coureur de bois*, Gabriel Ferry
	Voyage au pays des peintres, Marie Proth
	Catalogue de la société des aquarellistes français
1880	*Chacun son idée*, Jules Girardin
	Chansons choisis, Gustave Nadaud
	Le Jour de l'an et les étrennes, Eugène Muller
	Les Drames du désert, Noir
1881	*En revenant de Pontoise*, H. le Charpentier
	L'Amérique septentrionale, Hippolyte Vattemare
1882	*La Chanson des nouveaux époux*, Mme Adam
	Life of George Cruikshank, Blanchard Jerrold
1883	*The Raven*, Edgar Allan Poe
	Catalogue de la société des aquarellistes français
1907	*Versailles et Paris en 1871*, Doré